de S...

hardie grant EGMONT

I Heart You, Archie de Souza
published in 2012 by
Hardie Grant Egmont
Ground Floor, Building 1, 658 Church Street
Richmond, Victoria 3121, Australia
www.hardiegrantegmont.com.au

All rights reserved. No part of this publication may be reproduced,
stored in a retrieval system or transmitted in any form by any means
without the prior permission of the publishers and copyright owner.

A CiP record for this title is available from the National Library of Australia

Text copyright © 2012 Chrissie Keighery
Illustration and design copyright © 2012 Hardie Grant Egmont

Design by Michelle Mackintosh
Text design and typesetting by Ektavo

Printed in Australia by Griffin Press, an Accredited ISO AS/NZS
14001:2004 Environmental Management System printer.

1 3 5 7 9 10 8 6 4 2

The paper this book is printed on is certified against the
Forest Stewardship Council® Standards. Griffin Press holds
FSC chain of custody certification SGS-COC-005088. FSC
promotes environmentally responsible, socially beneficial
and economically viable management of the world's forests.

FSC
www.fsc.org
MIX
Paper from
responsible sources
FSC® C009448

I Heart You, Archie de Souza

Chrissie Keighery

hardie grant EGMONT

'Who are we seeing first, Edi?' Dad asks.

I look at my sheet, then around the hall. All the teachers are sitting at desks with name placards in front of them.

'Mr Cartwright is first,' I say. 'Maths.' I point to where Mr C is sitting with a parent in front of him. Dad frowns and looks at his watch. He's about the only dad here in a suit and tie.

'Time?' he asks.

'Five-thirty until five-forty,' I say.

Dad shakes his head. Mr Cartwright's a bit behind

schedule. Four minutes behind, so far, but that's enough to get Dad annoyed.

'Hey, Edi!' Hazel calls from across the room. She's with her mum and her mum's boyfriend. Hazel reckons he's always trying to take an interest in her and she wishes he would leave it alone – but I think it's cute. He has long dreadlocks and he's wearing purple pants. As they walk towards us, I see that his pants are covered in paint splatters. I try to imagine my dad dressed like that and it almost makes me laugh.

'Hi, Edi,' says Hazel's mum. 'Hi,' she says to Dad. 'I'm Diana.'

'This is my dad,' I say to Hazel's mum.

'Hi, Edi's dad,' Hazel's mum says, smiling and holding out her hand.

'Graeme,' Dad says with a handshake.

'Jason,' the boyfriend joins in. He holds out his hand and I can tell he's surprised by how firm Dad's handshake is.

'So, how's Edi going at school?' Hazel's mum asks. 'Is she keeping out of trouble?'

She says it lightly, to be funny, but my dad doesn't get

that kind of thing. He pulls my report out of the pocket inside his suit coat and looks over his shoulder. Mr Cartwright is still talking to the same parent.

'Hmm,' is all Dad says. My report wasn't so great. Well, it was less than perfect. Which, in my house, means no good. My family are all brainiacs. Dad is a surgeon, Mum's a lawyer. I have a brother, Jai, who's way older than me. He's studying medicine. No pressure.

'Come on, Edi,' Dad says. I follow him. I don't have a good feeling about this. Mr C is running seven minutes behind schedule now.

'Excuse me,' Dad interrupts the conversation Mr C is having with Alice's parents. 'I believe my interview was for five-thirty.'

'I'll just finish up here,' Mr C replies calmly. 'I'm sure we won't be long.'

Dad steps away. 'Not good enough,' he says under his breath.

I cringe and hope Mr C didn't hear. He does a double take, like he thought he heard what Dad said, and then decided he must have been wrong. I can see Hazel, her mum and Jason introducing themselves to Mr Brennan, our SOSE teacher. Hazel's mum is smiling and nodding, like a normal parent.

'Hello, Mr Rhineheart,' says a voice.

I turn and see it's Pip, my drama teacher. My favourite teacher. She's really into her subject. Half our other teachers basically hate students, but Pip actually seems to like us.

'I can see you while you're waiting for Mr Cartwright, if you like,' she offers.

Dad crosses his arms. 'What subject do you teach?' he asks.

'Drama,' she replies. She points over to her table, indicating that we should go and sit down.

Dad doesn't move. 'Hmmm, I'll come over if we have time,' he says. Translated from Dadspeak, that means, *Why would I bother talking to you about a useless subject like drama?*

I got the top marks for drama in our whole class, but that's not counted in our house. I'd like to make myself disappear.

Pip tilts her head to the side and gives me a little smile. 'Edi is showing quite a talent for drama. She has real presence, and an ability to inhabit a character with depth and feeling. I think she has a good chance of getting a lead role in the school play next year.'

I cringe a little, but I guess it's nice Pip said that. And it's funny to watch Dad's reaction. His eyebrows go so high they're practically off his face. Jai can imitate that face perfectly. He even put a photo of himself doing it on Facebook, captioned 'Dadface'. Just for me.

'Yes, well,' Dad says. 'She's quite the drama queen at home too.'

Pip smiles like she thinks Dad has made a joke, but he hasn't, of course. He was being serious. She opens her mouth to say something more, but Dad's spotted that the parent Mr C was busy with is now getting up to go. I smile apologetically at Pip as we head over to Mr C's table.

'Sorry to keep you waiting,' Mr C says as we sit down. Dad doesn't say anything to this. Mr C looks at his book, which has all my marks for tests and whatever. 'Edi has performed quite solidly this year,' he begins.

Dad studies my report card. 'Not solidly enough,' he counters.

Mr C nods. 'It's true that Edi could do better with a bit more application,' he says. 'She does tend to get distracted by …' Mr C looks like he's about to go on. I shoot him my very best, most *dramatic* pleading look. If he tells Dad about how Hazel and I got a detention for writing notes in class, or even worse, writing notes about boys in class, I'm a goner. '… things,' Mr C finishes, and even though he's strict I like him more now than I ever have. He's actually quite nice, I suddenly decide. 'Edi seems to have established some good friendsh–'

'Should we get her a tutor?' Dad interrupts. He wants to get back on track. Friendships are not what school's for.

'Oh, I don't think that's necessary,' Mr C replies. 'Edi is in the top twenty-five per cent of the class. I believe she will be able to do better than that with a bit more application.'

Dad taps his mouth with the index finger of his left hand, like he's trying to decide whether to say more. The top twenty-five per cent means nothing to him. Jai was at the top, full stop.

Mr C continues talking. I see Jess waving at me from in front of Pip's table. I wave back. Jess is one of our crew, along with Olympia, Hazel and me. Her mum is laughing at something Pip's said, and I notice that she's rubbing Jess's back as she chats to Pip.

Dad's sitting next to me, but the thirty centimetres between us might as well have been measured with a ruler.

We move on to my science teacher, who says pretty much the same things Mr C said about me getting distracted. Then English. Dad cuts that one short, because there's nothing much to say when my marks are good. Only when they're not so good.

As soon as we get into the car to go home, Dad starts on me.

'It's a matter of focus, Edi,' he says. 'Nobody ever got anywhere by allowing themselves to be distracted when they should have been paying attention. We'll make a study timetable at home, so you can fit in homework around your rostered chores.'

'Mmm,' I say.

There's no point arguing with Dad. I already do more chores than any of my friends. At least when Jai still lived at home he used to make it fun to cook or put the rubbish out. Our driveway is really long and on bin night, I'd get a head start with the regular bin while he took the recycling. It was basically anything goes. You could trip the other one up, or freak them out with stories of zombies hiding in the bushes. The winner was whoever got their bin to the road first.

Mostly, I won.

Mostly, Jai let me win.

'You don't get anywhere in life unless you …'

I tap the Clock app on my iPhone. It's beside my knee so Dad can't see. It's 4 a.m. this morning – Wednesday morning – in New York. It's so weird that Jai wouldn't have started his day yet while mine's nearly over.

'… no excuse for getting distracted …' It's a relief when Dad's phone rings. It's the hospital. Surprise, surprise. Dad takes the call on speakerphone. It's something about a patient of his who's in intensive care. I look out the window.

It's true that I've been distracted in class a lot lately, but I have a good reason. Archie de Souza. He's so hot and I *know* he likes me. I can tell by the way he looks at me. Other people have told me, too. The thing is, he's liked me for ages and he still hasn't done anything about it. So, just about every day, I have to plan how to run into him accidentally – which can be distracting. If I was actually going out with him, I wouldn't have to do that anymore. It's seriously frustrating. Especially now that Hazel is going out with his friend Leo.

Archie and Leo are both in the year above us. A while ago, Archie asked me and Hazel to his birthday party. It was pretty cool, but nothing really happened between Archie and me at the party, except that I got to sit on his knee for a round of truth or dare. Ever since then, I've been waiting for *something* to happen – for him to ask me out. Honestly, I thought Archie would ask me before Leo asked Hazel. But I'm still waiting.

Dad goes on about medications and stuff. The world passes by my window.

Maybe I should *stop* waiting? Maybe I should be the

one to ask him? Archie is hot, but I think he's also shy. It could take him forever to ask me.

It's tradition that the boy asks the girl. But it's not like I'm really into tradition.

It's possible that he could say no, I guess. But maybe he's thinking the same thing – that *I* could say no.

My mind keeps swinging between the alternatives.

Ask him. Wait. Ask him. Wait.

It's really annoying. Normally, I'm pretty quick to make decisions. I totally hate waiting.

I guess it's one of those things that might become clearer if I talk about it with my friends. If he hasn't done anything by Friday, I'll ask the caravan crew what they think.

Two

By Friday afternoon, I've hardly even seen Archie. Unless seeing him at a distance while he's playing soccer counts.

When I get home from school, I check the roster of chores on the fridge. It's my turn to tidy the kitchen so Mum has a clean bench to start dinner when she gets home. Plus, even though it's not on the roster, I have to do a load of washing or I'll be undie-less for the weekend.

I'm cleaning up the caravan when Olympia arrives. She's fifteen minutes early.

'Hi, Limps,' I say over my shoulder. I'm putting up the

picture I found at the op shop yesterday. 'Can you hold this for me?'

I hammer in the picture hook while Olympia holds the picture.

We step back to look at it after I've finished. It's a white cloud in the shape of a heart, floating through a blue sky. I wanted to have it up before everyone came.

'It looks great, Edi,' Olympia says, nudging me. 'Just like I knew it would. I can't wait to get mine up above my bed. It looks so romantic.'

Olympia went to the op shop with me, and she walked straight past the picture. It was only when I picked it up that she paid any attention to it. Then she came over and saw it was one of a pair. The second picture had the same cloud floating in the opposite direction. Limps started talking about how cool it would be to have one each, so in the end we both bought one. But I totally remember she said she was going to put hers above her desk. I know I should just forget about it, but sometimes her copying does annoy me.

She's right, though. It does look great above my bed.

We're both still looking at it when I hear footsteps. It's Hazel and Jess.

'Oh my god,' Jess says, peeking her head into the caravan. 'That looks awesome!' She walks up the steps and flings herself on the bed. 'I'm so glad we've got the meeting tonight,' she says. 'Luke has about a thousand stinky little mates over at our place. Honestly, the whole house pongs. There's nowhere to get away from them.'

'We got the picture from the op shop down the road,' Olympia says, even though no-one's asked about it. 'It was one of a pair, and I got the other one.'

I have a feeling Olympia wants the others to know that we did something together, just the two of us. And that we have matching pictures to prove it. Limps is funny like that.

'It's cool,' Hazel says vaguely. She sits down next to Jess. 'It's good to get out of my place as well. Jason and Mum are meditating. Right in the middle of the lounge room. I can't even watch TV!' She puts her hands out to either side, her index finger and thumb touching. Then she goes cross-eyed. 'Om, om, om,' she chants.

Hazel always makes us laugh.

I try to imagine my parents sitting on the lounge room floor, going *ommm*. It's higher up the unlikely-to-ever-happen list than Dad wearing purple pants and growing dreadlocks. You'd think, with Mum being Indian and all, that she might be into meditating. But her work is her life. She's as boring as Dad.

'Honestly, Edi,' Jess says, sitting up on my bed. 'You're so lucky to have this caravan.'

'Well,' Olympia replies, though Jess was talking to me, 'Edi's parents respect her privacy.'

I just shrug. My parents bought the caravan about the time Jai decided to go to New York to study. He won a scholarship to study medicine there. As you do.

When he left, I felt as if there was a giant hole in our family. But at least the caravan was there, promising something good to come. As soon as I finished primary school, Mum, Dad and I were going to take off. Mum and Dad were *finally* going to take holidays, and we were going to roam around. Explore. Spend time at the beach or in funny little towns. I told myself, I *convinced* myself, that my brother moving out didn't mean the end of our family.

But three days into our trip, Dad got called into work. He resisted. Then five days in, Mum got a similar call. I was really upset and I let them know, but there was no real debate. They both chose their jobs.

Since then, the caravan has just sunk into the backyard. We've never even pretended to plan another trip. I don't mention the idea. There's a lot I don't mention to my parents. There's no point. So, in a way, Olympia is right. I certainly get plenty of privacy these days. If that's what you want to call it.

I try to think about something else, something I might be able to change. I clap my hands. 'We have an agenda,' I say brightly.

'Oh good!' Jess says. 'I love agendas.'

Hazel's grin is contagious. 'Depending on what they are, of course,' she says.

Jess giggles. 'Yep, depending on what they are.' But I don't think she actually knows what Hazel means.

The three of them squeeze into the lime-green bench seats around the kitchen table. I stand.

'Point one,' I say. 'Do you think Archie de Souza likes me?'

'Totally,' Olympia says.

Jess nods so enthusiastically that her ringlets bounce up and down.

'He does,' Hazel says. 'Leo told me.'

'Oh my god,' Jess says suddenly. 'If you two got together, you'd be the hottest couple around!'

'Thanks, Jess,' Hazel says.

'Oh, soz! No offence,' Jess says quickly.

Since Hazel and Leo are definitely a couple and they've been together for three whole weeks, it's not the smartest comment in the world. But I can tell Hazel's not really offended. That's just Jess.

'Okay, point two,' I continue. I take a deep breath. 'He still hasn't asked me out.' Everyone nods, so I move on to the next point. 'Point three. I'm wondering whether I should ask him. If I don't, it might never happen.'

'Totally!' Olympia practically yells it and it's way before she's had time to really think about it properly.

I watch Hazel's face. She screws up her nose and bites

her lip but she doesn't say anything.

'You should, Edi,' Jess says. 'It would be like in this movie I saw where the guy thought he wasn't good enough for the girl because he'd done something wrong and I can't remember what he did wrong but he couldn't get up the guts to ask her to marry him, so the girl waits for a leap year, which is when it's okay to break tradition and a girl can ask a guy out, and she gets down on her knees, and I think they were at the beach but they might have been –'

Olympia and Hazel both put their right hand up in a *stop-right-there* gesture. We've had to develop a quick way to get Jess back onto the planet when she goes off course.

'Oops,' Jess says, running her index finger and thumb over her lips and zipping them.

'Actually,' Hazel says slowly, 'Jess has a point with that story.'

'Do I?' Jess says with a grin.

'Well, I just mean it is sort of *traditional* that the boy asks the girl.' I know Hazel is weighing up the argument aloud, in her balanced way. She's about to continue when Olympia interrupts her.

'Yeah, in the olden days!' Olympia says sharply.

'Girls can ask boys out now. Can't we?' Jess ventures.

'The boy might say no,' I interject.

'So? How is that different to when a boy asks a girl?' Jess says, looking confused.

Hazel nods. 'That's true,' she says. 'Boys must feel bad when they ask a girl out and she says no.'

'This is stupid,' Olympia says really loudly. 'As if Archie would say no to Edi. Like, who wouldn't want to go out with the number one –'

Olympia stops herself, but we all know what she was about to say. We made a pact to never mention the 'hot list' that some guys at school made a while back. It was a list of the hottest girls in our year. We don't talk about it partly because it was just stupid, but also because this loser Nelson wrote something nasty next to Hazel's name on the list. I'm sure Hazel's over it now, but Limps is still a bit obsessed. Anyway, it really has nothing to do with this since Archie wasn't even involved in making the list.

'Who wouldn't want to go out with you?' Limps corrects herself.

It's nice that she says that, but Limps will say anything if that's what she thinks I want to hear. The fact is, she doesn't know Archie, so what she thinks has really just come through me. I want to hear Hazel's final opinion. She's the only one who's actually going out with someone. And the someone she's going out with is one of Archie's best friends.

'What do you think, Haze?' I prompt.

Hazel scratches her head. 'Like I told you, I know Archie likes you. I also know he's quite shy, and that's probably why he hasn't asked you yet. The other thing is that Leo tells me Archie's super busy with soccer. He trains three nights a week and plays on Sundays. So, maybe he's worried he might not have time for a girlfriend, you know?'

I think about it. It's pretty good news, actually. 'If that's why Archie hasn't asked me out yet, that's not such a big deal,' I say, trying to convince myself. At least Hazel thinks he likes me. 'So, do you think it's okay for girls to ask guys out?'

I'm kind of hoping for yes or no answers, but it's not what I get.

'Karen Leopold asked Bruno Lars,' Jess declares.

'Jeez, Jess,' Olympia says. 'That's a tragic example, since she's about two hundred kilos and he's a complete hottie. He ran away from her when she asked! I think Edi may have a bit more of a chance than Karen, hey?' Olympia is on a roll. 'I'd so do it if I were you, Edi,' she says. 'I mean, *you* would never seem desperate.'

I'm pretty sure Olympia wouldn't ask a guy out herself, so it's weird that she expects me to. Sometimes it seems like she's more plugged into my life than her own. But she also seems to think I'm totally different to everyone else, like I have some sort of immunity against getting hurt. Which I don't. I have my fair share of feeling crappy – not that anyone really knows about that.

If I actually managed to work up the courage to ask Archie and he said no, that would definitely hurt. I would feel like a complete loser. But I've been waiting *forever*.

'Maybe you should try to set things up so you spend some more time with him?' Hazel suggests. 'Then you could see how you feel. You could wait until he asks, if that feels right, or you could just ask him when you feel ready?'

Olympia rolls her eyes. 'Yeah, Edi should just sit back and wait while life passes her by,' she says.

But I can see that Hazel's idea is a good one, even if I am sick of waiting around. Maybe Archie and I need to spend some time together, and things will happen naturally.

'Actually, I think I like Hazel's idea,' I say. I can almost see Olympia's mind reversing over her last comment.

'We could find out when Alice is going to catch up with Archie next, and then you could just happen to be there,' Olympia says.

Alice hangs out with us sometimes and she's a family friend of Archie's. I think she'd be cool with it, but that could take ages. I'm starting to wonder if this will work.

'Or I could go and tell him that you like him,' continues Olympia, 'and that you want him to ask you out.'

Hazel looks squirmy. That's how I feel too. It's pretty babyish to do it that way. It's the sort of thing we used to do in primary school.

A better idea jumps into my head. 'Are you seeing Leo over the weekend?' I ask Hazel.

Hazel shrugs. 'We haven't planned anything, but we

might hang out at the skate park tomorrow,' she says. 'Sometimes we do that.'

That's another thing with Hazel. Most of the kids in our year who are going out with someone just avoid that person. It's like, as soon as they're boyfriend and girlfriend, everything gets awkward. Like, when I was going out with Oscar Poulson earlier in the year, we hardly spent any time together. Except at the blue-light disco, and that was more about hooking up than hanging out.

But Hazel and Leo actually hang out together. Maybe it's because Leo is a bit older. Archie is a bit older too … and tomorrow is Saturday, which means he won't be playing soccer.

'Why don't you text Leo and see if he can get Archie to go to the skate park, too?' I say.

I look around the table. Jess and Hazel are smiling, but Limps isn't. She's probably not happy that I didn't go with one of her ideas, but I think this is the way to go.

'And you could come along with me, I suppose?' Hazel says with a grin.

'Thanks for asking, Hazel. I might just be free,' I say.

Jess and I lean over Hazel's shoulder as she texts Leo. When I glance over at Limps, she has her arms crossed and a grumpy look on her face. Like she's being left out when, actually, she could come and stand with us if she wanted to.

'Limps, come and check the message before Hazel sends it,' I say.

She gets up straight away and comes over. Just like I thought, she doesn't look grumpy anymore. It's pretty easy to snap Limps out of her little moods.

Hazel presses send. It's done.

Three

For any normal teenager, it would be easy to make it out the door by 11 a.m. on a Saturday. But Saturday mornings in our house are one long, fun session of chores for everyone. I have to clean both the bathrooms while Mum vacuums and Dad mops the floorboards. By the time I finish, I'm late to meet Hazel.

'You smell like … Pine O'Cleen, or something,' Hazel says as we walk to the skate park.

I groan. 'I hope Archie doesn't notice,' I say. Hazel reaches into her backpack, pulls out a bottle of perfume and sprays me on the wrist. Lifesaver.

'So, are you actually going to ask him?' she says. 'Like, how? Are you nervous? What will you say?'

I thought about this last night before I went to sleep. I decided if Archie doesn't do it today, then I will. I wasn't nervous then, but I do feel a bit wobbly now. *Just stick to the plan,* I tell myself.

'What's the plan?' Hazel asks as though she's read my mind.

'Okay,' I say. I go in front of Hazel and walk backwards so I can see her reaction properly. 'The four of us will be sitting at one of the bench tables at the skate park. You and Leo will be chatting like you always do and Archie and I will get a chance to talk. Right?' I ask.

'Good so far,' Hazel confirms.

'So, after a while, when we're all sort of relaxed, I'll give a signal for you to take Leo away and leave me and Archie alone.'

'What's the signal?' Hazel asks.

'Hmmm,' I say. 'How about I kick you under the table?'

'As in, gently,' Hazel says with a giggle.

'Of course,' I say and I must be more nervous than I think because when I think about kicking Hazel under the table I get the giggles.

'So, you'll be alone with Archie and then what will you say?' Hazel asks when we recover.

'How about, "Will you marry me?"' I say. It feels good to be the funny one for a change and we both crack up all over again.

'Perfect,' Hazel says.

We still have the giggles when we arrive at the skate park. It's a nice, sunny day, not too hot or too cold, and there are loads of people. First of all, I notice that all of the tables and bench seats are taken. It looks like people are really settling in because there's food on each table and the smell of barbecue in the air. If I'd known that, I would have brought a picnic rug. *So much for my plan.*

'Leo's over there,' Hazel says, pointing. I look to where heaps of skaters are doing turns and tricks on the ramp. Then I spot Leo. He isn't skating, he's leaning against the graffiti wall. Archie doesn't seem to be with him. Hazel waves and we walk around the ramp towards Leo.

'Hey, Hazardous. Hey, Edi,' says Leo, and it's pretty cute how he reaches for Hazel's hand and holds it. With his free hand, Leo points a finger and moves it along. It takes me while to get what he's pointing at because the ramp is so crowded. But then I see.

Archie is an awesome skater. He twists his way through all the others and comes up the lip of the ramp. His skateboard flies over the top and then he turns it around and flies back to the other end.

'Pretty cool, hey?' Leo says. 'You know, Archie only had that board for a few months. He never even skated before that.'

'He's a freak,' Hazel agrees. I'd like to say something but I'm too busy watching Archie. He's wearing a yellow T-shirt, which is my favourite colour, and when he moves I can see the muscles in his arms.

'Do you skate?' I finally ask Leo, my eyes still glued to the Archie show.

'Nah, Archie's the sporty one,' he says. Then he grins and looks at Hazel. 'I'm the smart, handsome, arty one,' he says.

'Don't forget modest,' Hazel says, taking her hand out of Leo's so she can give him a little punch in the arm.

'So, which one's your latest?' Hazel asks Leo.

'This one,' Leo replies, gesturing to a weird picture of a girl in a bikini with a sash that says, 'Miss Everything'. She has super-sized feet. Underneath, he's written, 'Filling the Big Shoes'.

'You like it?' he asks.

'Yep,' I say. To be honest, I don't really even get it, but Leo's not listening to me anyway. It's Hazel's opinion he's after.

'It's great,' I hear Hazel say, but when the two of them start talking about how he painted it for her, I zone out and keep watching Archie. It's been a while. I wonder if he knows we're here. That I'm here. I test it by waving. Archie waves back. Then he keeps skating. The tricks are getting a bit repetitive.

'If it's up to Archie, he'll be out there for another hour,' Leo says when he and Hazel have finished their latest loved-up chat. He must've noticed that I'm getting impatient. 'Don't take it personally, Edi. Seriously, he just gets carried away. But I know a trick to get him here if you're up for it.'

Actually, I didn't think I'd need a trick. But Archie isn't showing any sign of stopping. 'Okay,' I say. 'What's the trick?'

'A caramel milkshake from the shop across the road will do it,' Leo grins. 'I'll go get one.'

Leo and Hazel go to the shop together and I'm left by myself at the side of the ramp. Things aren't exactly going the way I'd planned. Then, suddenly, Archie flicks his skateboard up, catches it and starts walking towards me.

'Hi, Edi,' he says. 'Um … sorry if I … um … took too long.' His skateboard is tucked under his arm and he's looking down and kicking the grass. It's so cute. It's weird to think how confident he looked while he was skating, because he's obviously nervous now.

'That's fine,' I say. 'You're really good.'

'Oh, well … um, thanks,' he says and finally he looks at me. 'Man! You look … um … nice today.' He taps his forehead. 'Oh, that sounds like you don't look good other days. Um … that's not how –'

'I know,' I say. 'Thanks.' I smile at him. The smile

he gives me back is so gorgeous I could get lost in it. Up close, I can see his yellow T-shirt is old. There's a section on the chest that's almost transparent, like the fabric's nearly worn through. I wonder if it's his favourite.

I don't say anything for a while. If I wait, maybe he'll ask me out and I won't have to ask him? That would be perfect.

But Archie doesn't say anything either. We're just kind of standing there. Then I see Leo and Hazel coming back from the shops. They *definitely* have things to talk about. I look at them and the way they're chatting makes us just standing here feel even more awkward. Archie spins the wheels of his skateboard.

'Skater boy!' Leo says when they reach us. 'Nice moves.' He hands Archie the milkshake. Hazel is carrying a parcel of hot chips.

'Thanks,' Archie mutters, balancing his board in one hand and milkshake in the other. When Hazel offers him a chip, Archie gives her a *how am I going to manage that?* look. It's seriously cute.

'Let's go sit over there,' Leo says.

It's not a bench seat like I planned, and the grass is a bit wet, but at least we find a spot and sit down in a row – Leo, Hazel, Archie, then me. Hazel shares her chips, and I have to lean across Archie to get more.

'Check out the little dude,' Archie says. He's pointing back at the skate ramp. To tell the truth, I'm a bit sick of watching and I wouldn't mind if we just talked between us for a while, but at least he's talking to me.

The little dude looks about six years old. He's wearing a stripy beanie and baggy jeans with his undies sticking out the top. It's a cute look, but full-on for a six-year-old. He jumps his board in the air every few metres.

'He's pretty good,' I say. 'But you're way better.'

Archie doesn't reply. Now I feel embarrassed about what I said. It probably sounded too keen or something. We seem to have stalled. Hazel and Leo break into the silence between Archie and me.

'You have to get to episode three,' Hazel is saying, 'that's when it gets really good.'

'Nah, don't think I'm going to make it there, Hazel. I'm just not into it.'

'Yeah, but you will be into it if you keep going,' Hazel insists. 'Remember, *persistence*, Leo!'

Leo grins. 'What about passion and zeal?' he asks.

I sneak a little smile at Archie and he smiles back. Our school motto is 'passion, zeal and persistence'.

'Yeah, while you're at it, get some *zeal* going too,' Hazel says, laughing.

'Zeal is very underrated,' Leo says. 'You keep forgetting passion though.'

Hazel puts her head on Leo's shoulder. 'No, I don't,' she says. Honestly, the two of them are so made for each other.

Some of their perfection must have rubbed off because Archie reaches out a hand and puts it on the small of my back. I've never really thought about the small of my back but it tingles where he touches it. I hope he never takes it away.

'Thanks ... er ... Edi,' he says, picking up from my comment about five minutes ago. 'I like skating, it's sort of a new hobby for me, but soccer is my main thing. Do you like soccer?'

His hand is still there. Hmmm.

'Yeah, soccer is great,' I say. It's only a little lie. In fact it might even be true. It's not that I like soccer or don't like soccer. It just hasn't been on my radar. But it *could* be. I search my mind for any little soccer fact that might have randomly got in. 'I like how nobody is allowed to touch the ball with their hands,' I say.

'Except the goalkeeper,' Archie says.

'Except the goalkeeper,' I agree, as though I already knew that.

Archie's hand has been on my back for all that time and he's looking me almost right in the eyes now and I have this funny feeling like he just might be going to ask me. Then his mobile rings. Archie takes his hand off my back and reaches into the pocket of his cargo shorts. He stands up and walks away to take the call. I shift closer to Hazel.

'How's it going?' she whispers, so Leo can't hear.

'I don't know,' I say. 'I had a feeling he was going to ask me, but then he got that call.' I shrug.

'Do you want to kick my leg?' Hazel asks. I'd almost forgotten about the under-the-table kick I'd planned. But Archie is so shy, maybe there would be more chance of him asking me out if Leo and Hazel went away for a while?

I lift my leg and give Hazel a little kick.

'Leo, let's go and look at the ducks,' Hazel says and she gets up and pulls Leo up by his hand and they go. I wait for Archie. Finally, he comes back.

'Sorry, Edi,' he says, 'that was … er … my cousin. He's been living with us but he's found a flat and he wants me to help him move out this afternoon. So I … um … better go.'

There's a little frown on Archie's forehead as he talks and, for a moment, I wonder if something is bothering him. I nearly ask if he's okay, but he's the first one to talk again.

'Where are Leo and Hazel?'

'They've gone down to the lake,' I say. I'm really hoping that Archie will sit down again and something might actually happen, but he picks up his skateboard. He seems like he's in a hurry to go.

'Can you say bye for me?' Archie says.

I make myself smile, even though I totally don't feel like smiling. 'Yeah, sure,' I say, standing up.

'Well, bye,' Archie says and that's going to be it. As in

nothing. It would be too weird for me to ask him now. Too random.

'Bye,' I say.

I watch Archie walk away, his skateboard tucked under his arm. I lie back on the grass, close my eyes and fling my arms over my head. Nothing has gone to plan. Not. One. Thing.

'Edi?'

I open my eyes. Archie is kneeling next to me. His head hovers over me. He's come back!

'I was … um … just wondering …' It's weird seeing Archie's face from this angle, but he must think *I'm* really weird, lying down on the grass like this. 'We've got soccer … um … semifinals tomorrow. Since you're into … er … soccer … I just … um … wondered if you'd like to … um … come along? We could sort of … catch up … after the game.'

I smile, and this time it's genuine. 'Yep, absolutely,' I say and I totally don't care about plans anymore because this is good. It's awesome.

'I'll text you the details then,' Archie says.

'Do you have my number?' I ask.

Archie nods and smiles and I don't know how he got my number but the fact that he has bothered to get it from someone is a good sign.

I can't wait until tomorrow!

Four

'Hi, Edi. I saved you a seat.' Alice says. She's wearing an oversized soccer T-shirt that makes her look like a boy. She's pretty clueless about stuff like that, but she's nice.

'Hello, love,' Archie's mum says. 'You look cold.' Before I know it, she's produced a blanket and spread it over my knees.

I'm not actually that cold, but it's a sweet thing to do.

'You ready for the big game?' Archie's dad asks. His accent is really strong. 'This team is beating us last time, but we're thinking *this* game is ours.'

'Yes, thanks, Mr de Souza,' I say. 'I'm ready.'

'Please, you are making me feel old. Call me Mario,' he says.

'You *are* old, Mario,' says Archie's mum.

It's so cute how Archie's dad shakes his finger at Archie's mum, then puts his arm around her. She wriggles out of the hug and reaches into the basket at her feet.

Next thing I know, I have a hot chocolate in one hand and a piece of orange cake in the other and the game has started. It goes on. And on. I don't know how everyone except for me stays so excited because it's ages before Archie's team scores a goal. And even longer before they score a second.

Archie's parents barrack loudly. Archie gets the ball a lot and he must be pretty good because there's lots of cheering when he does.

'He's like Beckham,' Alice says to me.

I nod. I'm pretty sure I know who Beckham is. 'Isn't that Posh Spice's husband?' I ask.

Alice laughs. 'No, Posh Spice is Beckham's wife.'

I giggle. 'I'm not sure about that, Alice,' I say. 'I'm pretty sure Posh is the one who has all the good outfits. And since she's most likely the one who chooses her husband's clothes and influences fashion all around the world, I think it's fair to say he is her husband, not the other way around.'

'Does she?' Alice says. Honestly, I don't think she knows anything about Posh.

'Yeah, totally,' I say. 'Like, the boyfriend jean for instance.' I point down at my jeans to show Alice.

'Aren't they just normal jeans?' Alice asks.

'Not really. They're a different fit. Kind of baggy, as though you've borrowed them from your boyfriend and they're a little bit big on you.'

'Oh,' Alice says and she stares at my jeans looking confused, like she's trying to figure out what's different about them.

But then there's a commotion on the soccer field and we both look up. The umpire is holding up something that looks like a swap card, but it's yellow.

'Oh my god,' Alice says, shaking her head. 'Pezza just got a yellow card.'

'Is that good?' I wonder aloud.

Alice turns to me. 'No, it's not good. It's a warning. If he gets another one he'll be sent off.'

'Oh,' I say. Now it's my turn to be the clueless one. Alice must notice my expression, and for a moment I feel really silly.

'I think you know as much about soccer as I know about fashion,' she says.

'Don't tell Archie that!' I almost squeal, but remember at the last moment to keep my voice down.

'I don't think he'd mind,' she says softly.

'Seriously, he can't know,' I whisper. The only thing Archie and I have in common so far is soccer and I totally don't want to lose that.

Alice gives me a little smile. 'Okay, Edi,' she says. 'How about I teach you a bit about soccer and you teach me a bit about fashion?'

I smile back. Alice is so nice. I'm not sure if she's making this deal because she really wants to know more about clothes and stuff, but I do get the feeling that she'll keep my secret anyway. She seems like someone you can trust.

V

Finally, the siren sounds and everyone stands up and cheers. Archie's team has won. I stand up and join them.

'It's very good result,' Mario says to me and Alice. 'Archie is a very big sack of sad when they lose.'

'Yep,' Alice agrees. 'Remember how he went to bed and stuck his head under the pillow for about two hours after they lost to this team last time?'

'I am remember,' Mario says and I feel a bit out of it because I am the only one who isn't *remembering*.

'Please come back to our house for dinner, Edi,' Archie's mum says, pulling me back into the loop. 'You must be starving by now.'

I'm definitely not starving. I've had two hot chocolates and three pieces of orange cake. But I do want to go back to Archie's place for dinner. His parents are so nice.

'That would be good, thanks,' I say.

As they pack up, I text Mum.

Is it okay if I go to Hazel's for dinner? Her mum can drop me home.

I'm not exactly sure whether Mum would let me go to Archie's for dinner. It would probably be okay since his parents will be there. During the week, I can only go to people's houses if it's to do with school work. I'm allowed to go out on Sunday nights as long as I'm home by nine. Then again, Archie is a boy. Telling the truth is too risky.

Yes. Be home by 9.

We're walking towards the car when Archie comes up. He's changed out of his soccer gear. His T-shirt is burnt orange, totally yummy against his olive skin and tight enough to see the shape of his muscles underneath. He is completely not a sack of sad. He punches his hand in the air. His mum squeezes his shoulders and kisses his cheeks on both sides. He rolls his eyes like he's embarrassed, but his grin is from ear to ear.

As soon as she lets him go, he picks me up and spins me around. As he does it, it reminds me of Jai whirring me around the backyard like a doll. Popping me down, totally dizzy, both of us laughing as I tried to stand straight.

When Archie puts me down, I kind of wish he'd do it

again. But he moves on to Alice. At least I can watch his muscles ripple as he spins her.

V

'This is the best gnocchi I've ever tasted,' I say. The table is totally stacked with food considering there's only four of us. We dropped Alice home on the way because she had a netball game.

'It's gnocchi primavera,' Archie's mum says. 'Very easy. I could teach you sometime.'

'That would be great,' I say. It's my turn to cook on Tuesday nights, but I just do boring stuff. Chops, vegies, that kind of thing. People sometimes think that because Mum is Indian, we might eat loads of yummy curries and stuff but Mum doesn't like the curry sauce that comes in jars from the supermarket and she thinks they take too long to make from scratch. There's no time for stuff like that in my house.

'You come for a cooking lesson anytime, Edi,' Archie's mum says. 'I'm in the kitchen every day from five o'clock.'

She spoons some more into my bowl. I'm so full I'm about to burst, but I eat it all because I can tell it's making her happy. I'm happy too, sitting next to Archie around his family table like this.

My family used to eat at the table when Jai was still home. Even though Mum and Dad were usually pretty serious, he made it fun. There were little games we'd play without Mum and Dad even catching on. 'Pea Store' was a goodie. You'd have to get right to the end of the meal and then wait until the table was cleared and Mum and Dad were finished in the kitchen and had gone to another room and then, finally, you revealed how many peas you'd stored under your tongue. My record was fourteen. Jai was the reigning champion with twenty-five, though I still reckon he cheated. By the time we'd waited for Mum and Dad to get out of the kitchen and got around to checking the mush in his mouth, it was more of an estimate than an actual pea count.

Now, with just the three of us, it just feels like there's no point setting the table. We mostly eat quickly at the bench so Mum and Dad can get back to work.

'My wife is the magnificent cook,' Mario says, kissing his fingers and releasing them. 'It's the reason I marry her.' He tilts his head to the side and looks at her. 'She is my *bella donna*,' he says.

'Dad. Embarrassing,' Archie says and he looks at me and shakes his head like he's apologising for his dad.

He doesn't need to. I don't know what *donna* means, but I know that *bella* means beautiful. Honestly, Archie's mum is nice and everything, but she's small and round and not really very pretty. Which kind of makes it more romantic that Mario thinks she is. My mum is actually good-looking, for someone her age, and my dad never says anything like that to her. My parents probably make a booking with each other for romance. Maybe it's in small print somewhere on the chores roster.

Archie's mum keeps refilling his bowl as soon as he's finished.

'Mum!' Archie says, as his mum hovers another spoonful of gnocchi over his bowl. She shakes her head.

'Rio could eat twice as much as you, Archie,' she says, gesturing with her free hand to the empty chair next to her.

'No, he couldn't,' Archie protests. It's funny. I don't know who Rio is, but Archie points to the empty chair just like his mum did. Obviously, whoever Rio is, that's his chair.

'Yes, he could. Rio could eat what you just ate as an afternoon snack and be ready for dinner an hour later,' Archie's mum argues, putting the gnocchi onto Archie's plate. Archie turns to me and rolls his eyes, but he keeps eating anyway.

There's lots of soccer talk while we finish. It's a bit boring, but I can zone out and watch Archie. His green eyes light up as he talks. Occasionally, when his smile reaches a certain point, dimples appear in his cheeks and then disappear like magic. His skin. His dark, wavy hair. His lips ...

'Just a little bit more, Edi?' Archie's mum interrupts my thoughts.

'Oh, no thanks,' I say. I look at the clock on the wall. It's 8.30. 'Can I help you clear up? Then I'd better go home.'

Archie gives me a questioning look, a *why would you*

ask that? look. I get the feeling he doesn't do much clearing up himself.

'No clearing up for the guest,' Mario says. He looks at me, then at Archie. 'This one is good,' he says. 'Polite and lovely too. You walk *quella* home, son.'

Yes, walk quella home, Archie, I think, though I have no idea what a *quella* is.

Soon, we're out in the night. Alone.

'That was a really great day,' Archie says as we walk. 'I can't believe we won. I reckon our team played the best soccer we've played for ages. Like, did you see the save our goalkeeper did? It was so Victor Valdés.'

It's funny. When Archie talks about soccer, he leaves out all the 'um's and 'er's. He seems so happy. I don't really get half of it, and I'm not that interested, but it's nice just listening to him talk about something he cares about. I can't wait until we know each other better. Until I find out other things he's passionate about. Then, there'll be loads of stuff to talk about that I'll really be able to get into.

'God, Edi. Sorry. I'm … um … going on and on. What were you thinking just then? You looked like you'd …

um … gone somewhere else.'

'Nothing,' I say. 'Just that I had a great day too. Thanks for asking me.' We keep walking, but slowly. Like neither of us really wants to get there. 'What does *quella* mean?' I ask. 'Your dad called me *quella*.'

Archie stops walking. I stop too and we sort of turn into each other. He shakes his head and, honestly, I think he's blushing. 'It means a few things,' he says.

'Like what?'

'Like … um … "that girl",' he says quietly, 'or … um … like, "the girl in his life".'

'*Quella*,' I say. I love the sound of it. I like the meaning too. *The girl in Archie's life.* I take a step closer to him. He puts his hands on my waist and we're looking right at each other.

Ask me. Ask me.

'Um, Edi?' he says.

'Yeah?'

'I was just … er … wondering …'

'Yes,' I say softly, hoping it encourages him.

'Would you … um … er … um … go out with me?'

My heart is skipping. A jump rope in my chest.

I lean into him and put my arms around his waist. His chest is broad. It absorbs the pumping in mine. My cheek rests against his, and feels soft where his is rough. Whatever I felt when he put his hand on my back is nothing compared to this. I move my head so my lips are on his lips. He has the best lips ever. Not too hard, not too soft. I love this kiss. I want to live inside this kiss. It's nothing like the kisses I had with Oscar Poulson at the blue-light disco. They were just baby stuff. This is *real*.

Archie pulls away first. 'So, is that a yes?' he asks.

'It's totally a yes,' I reply.

V

'So, how was Hazel's?' Mum asks. Dad is asleep on the couch. Mum's sitting next to him in one of the armchairs. She's wearing her old-person's glasses and has an open book in her hands.

'Good,' I say. I'm still floating. In that kiss. In my new life as Archie de Souza's girlfriend.

'What did you have for dinner?' she asks.

'Gnocchi,' I reply. 'Gnocchi primavera.' I say it with an Italian accent but Mum doesn't seem to notice.

'That's nice,' Mum says. 'I hope you've done all your homework. And have you got your uniform and everything ready for tomorrow?'

'I'm ready for tomorrow,' I say. I've never been more ready for a Monday. If I could go to school right now, I would. Just to see Archie again. 'Absolutely.'

Five

As if it isn't already bad enough to have a double maths period first thing on Monday morning, Mr C is on my back. It's all, 'Where are you up to, Edi?' and 'Keep your focus, Edi,' which is totally not fair.

Nick gets away with being really noisy as usual and I know he can't really help it because of his Down syndrome, but there are definitely double standards in this classroom. Heaps of other kids get away with talking too. I bet Dad freaked Mr C at the parent–teacher interview.

I get through two whole pages of the textbook, which

puts me in front of everyone else at my table. When I get to chapter six, Mr C moves me to Alice's table because she's the only other girl who's up to it.

Alice is really keen and she never gets distracted. It's a bit boring, but I don't really care about being moved. I told the girls that Archie and I are together and they keep hassling me to go through every little detail of how it happened. It's nice just having some bits to myself. Or between Archie and me anyway.

V

'Who's coming down to the tree?' I ask at lunchtime when we're at the lockers. I reckon Archie will be there. He normally plays soccer but I'm pretty sure that today will be different, seeing as we're going out together now.

'Not me,' Hazel says. 'I don't really like it down there, Edi. And I'm going to meet up with Leo at the canteen.'

'Me too,' Jess says and launches into a long explanation about why she wants to hang out with Leo and Hazel. I don't really listen because I know she's just being a chicken. Everyone down at the tree is from the year above us and some of the girls aren't very friendly.

'I'll come with you,' Limps says. Olympia can get a bit annoying sometimes, but she's always there for me.

There are actually no guys down at the tree. Just the girls who always hang out at the bench. As we walk past them, Eliza, the girl who organised truth or dare at Archie's party, is talking. When she sees us, she stops speaking and gives us a look. A definite *what do you think you're doing here?* look.

Olympia and I ignore her, and lean against the tree, waiting for Archie to show. We can hear Eliza from here, though we can't see her face.

'Anyway,' she says, 'so, everyone's been hassling Nelson to show them some proof.'

I catch on to what she's on about. I remember Nelson bragging about hooking up with some really hot girl when we played truth or dare at Archie's party.

'So,' Eliza continues, 'he shows Pezza this photo on his laptop and Pezza copies and pastes it and writes "Nelson's Fling" at the bottom and forwards it to everyone.'

'Yeah, I got that photo,' someone says. 'I have to admit, she was pretty hot. And did you *see* that white bikini?'

'Der,' Eliza says, '*everybody* got it. But the thing is that one of the guys had seen that shot on the net. It was a Victoria's Secret model!'

'Oh, so she wasn't his girlfriend after all,' someone says.

Eliza groans. 'Thanks for that, Captain Obvious,' she says, harshly. I have a feeling that the other girl might be a bit like Jess, as in a bit slow to get things sometimes. 'Anyway, now everyone knows what a loser Nelson is,' Eliza concludes.

Even though I don't like Nelson, since he was the idiot who wrote something nasty about Hazel on the hot list, I actually feel a bit sorry for him.

Olympia speaks up. 'Nelson wrote something horrible about a friend of ours.' I'm shocked she says that.

Eliza swings around and gives us a foul look that has Olympia taking a step backwards and practically jamming herself against the tree. 'Are you *kids* still here?' Eliza says.

I wish Olympia hadn't drawn attention to us, but I'm annoyed at Eliza calling us kids. It's so patronising.

'We're waiting for Archie,' I say. I can feel Olympia bristling next to me.

'Edi's going out with him,' Olympia says, taking that step forward to stand beside me again.

'Congratulations,' Eliza says sarcastically, and when she gets up and walks towards me I feel like it's going to be on. I'm not going to back away from her anyway. I make sure I'm standing very straight and I'm pleased that I'm actually taller than her, even though she's older.

'Of course, I already knew that,' she says. 'I know everything about Archie because he tells me. We hang out together all the time.' She narrows her eyes and puts a hand on her hip. 'We spend, like, so much time together now that we're doing this intense project for our science elective.' She drops her hand. 'There's no point trying to explain it to you. You'll get to it next year.'

'He tells Edi everything too,' Olympia says, and I'm surprised watching little Limps rev up for me. She has both her hands on her hips and her face is red.

'Oh, is that right?' Eliza says. She rolls her eyes at Olympia and then looks at me.

'So why don't you know that he never comes to the tree on Mondays? Why don't you know he plays soccer at lunchtime every day except Thursday?'

I actually did know that. I just thought it might be different now that we're going out together.

'Maybe because Edi isn't a stalker?' Olympia says under her breath and now she's really done it. Eliza's eyes go so narrow that they almost don't exist. I seriously can't help myself. I just burst out laughing.

'Hey, Edi. What's so funny?' I turn around and Archie's there.

'Oh, it's nothing. Just something Limps said,' I say.

'Ah, I just finished a soccer match and … I thought I'd come to the tree for the rest of … um … and you're here!' He sounds happy to see me and I can't resist giving Eliza a last glance. He doesn't even say hello to her.

'That's okay, Archie,' I say. 'I just thought you might be here.' Archie looks a bit confused, and, to be honest, I don't think that meeting up with me at lunchtime was high on his list. But it will be now.

It's kind of satisfying when Eliza slips away without

another word. There are only a few minutes until the bell goes, but if whatever was going on between me and Eliza was a competition, I've won. Well, I've won the first round anyway, which is weird because I actually haven't said a word to her.

One thing's for sure. I haven't heard the last of Eliza.

Six

At lunchtime the next day, I scope out the tree from the slopes next to the basketball courts rather than heading down there. I'm with the caravan crew and Leo. It's pretty cool how Leo hangs out with us half the time. I wish *someone else* would. I can see the bench girls hanging around near the tree, but no Archie.

'Is Archie playing soccer?' I ask Leo. He takes an Oreo from Hazel's lunchbox and she slaps him on the wrist.

'You've had *three*,' Hazel protests, 'show me what you've got to swap with.'

Leo laughs. 'You can have my carrot,' he offers, and gets another slap. He still hasn't answered me. Sometimes, it's like the two of them are in their own little universe.

'Is Archie playing soccer?' I ask again.

'Yeah,' Leo replies and now the two of them are taking alternate bites of the carrot. 'You won't get him off the soccer field, Edi. Especially not with the grand final coming up. He's in training.'

'Oh, that's cool,' I say, trying to make it sound casual. But I can't help feeling annoyed. I've barely seen him since Sunday.

'You know,' Leo continues, his mouth full of carrot, 'he trains right near your house on Tuesday arvos.'

I think about that all afternoon. I need to see him. Straight after school, I text Mum.

Can I have friend over for dinner 2nite? He's helping me with maths.

I know she'll go for it. I'm not allowed to do social stuff on a school night but anything to do with school work will get her in. As soon as she replies yes, I text Archie.

Drop into my place for dinner after training?

He's quick to respond.

Yep. Cool x

I love how he's added a kiss. I run my finger over it. And even though I'm worried Mum and Dad will be weird, I'm so excited.

I'll finally get to see my boyfriend.

I try not to race to the door when I hear a knock. That would make my parents suss.

'Hey, Edi.' There must be a shower at Archie's training ground. His dark hair is damp and kind of slicked back. He's wearing a green T-shirt that's almost the colour of his eyes, and he looks cute in his black skinny jeans. Maybe he's put on aftershave, or it might just be deodorant, but he smells amazing. It's hard to keep my distance.

'Hey, you,' I say. I wish I had time to explain that he has to pretend to be here to help me with maths, but Mum's already calling us to the table. The food is in the centre of the table, so we can just help ourselves. We all sit down.

'It's kind of you to help Edi with maths,' Mum says. 'Edi tells me you're a year ahead. So I guess you did what she's up to last year?'

I answer quickly so Archie will get it. 'Yes, it's really nice of you, Archie,' I say.

'We'd be happy to pay you for your time,' Dad pipes up. 'We were thinking of getting Edi a tutor anyway. So, what were your results?'

Seriously, it's like an interview. Archie doesn't know what to say. 'Um, well … there's no need …'

'Archie topped the year,' I say. I actually don't know anything about how Archie does in maths, so it *could* be the truth.

'That's good,' Dad says. 'That's good. So, do you know what you'd like to do when you leave school, Archie? Maths is definitely one of those subjects that opens doors.'

Archie swallows a mouthful of steamed vegies. The vegies are okay, but I can't help thinking of the gnocchi primavera his mum made. And of the way Archie's parents talked *normally*, not like they were scoping me out.

'Um, I'm actually … I mean, I'd like to … um … be a

professional soccer player,' he says.

Dad's eyebrows raise right up. Dadface. 'That's interesting,' he says. Which means *crazy* in Dadspeak. 'And what do your parents think of that?'

'Mum reckons I'll get there no problem, but Dad thinks I need to spend time working on my head ball. Sometimes I don't get the positioning right and then it doesn't come off at the right angle,' Archie says, and I can tell he has no clue that Dad thinks soccer is not a proper ambition. I need to rescue him. Luckily, he's almost finished his food.

'We're going to work in the caravan. All my books are there,' I say. I always do my homework in the caravan, so Mum and Dad just nod.

When we get to the caravan, Archie stands in the doorway and looks around. Then he shakes his head. I get the feeling there are a few things he wants to say and he's not sure what to start with.

'It's really nice in here, Edi,' he begins. I already know

what's coming. 'Um ... why did you tell your parents I was tutoring you? I mean ... I'm okay with maths but I ... er ... didn't top the class or anything. So, if you need help –'

'It's just easier, Archie,' I say. I take a deep breath and try to explain. 'It's just ... my mum and dad aren't like your mum and dad. I don't know if they'd be okay with me going out with you.'

'They seem nice,' Archie says with a shrug. 'Like, they seem okay, anyway. And my parents really like you. They said so. So, I don't see why –'

'Don't worry about it,' I say. He won't get it. He won't get how much pressure my parents put on me. Why would he? His own parents are so warm, they're like an open fire. Mine are more like an iceberg.

I sit on my bed and Archie finally follows me in. I pat a spot next to me. He moves aside a couple of cushions and sits too. The cloud picture is above us.

'My parents are really different to yours,' I say.

'Yeah, maybe,' he says, 'but don't you think it's better just to try to be ... well ... honest? I mean, sometimes

I think my mum or my dad won't understand something but then they ... kind of do.'

I tilt my head and look into those green eyes. There are dark flecks in there that I haven't noticed before. I don't know if Archie notices something new about me too, or if he's just got a glimpse of how sad I feel at home these days, but he puts his arms around me and pulls me to him.

'I can't. I can't be honest with them.' I don't know how to explain it to him. Of course, I talk to Mum and Dad, but they never listen properly. They listen with their ears, not with their hearts. It's as if everything they don't understand about me has built up into this big weight that sits on my chest.

I let my head sink into Archie's chest and rest there. I melt into him, feeling the beat of his heart on my cheek. It's like getting lost, but not somewhere bad. It's like getting lost in paradise.

We don't talk.

We don't need to.

I lift up my head so our faces are close together.

'You okay, Edi?' he asks. Those lips. I kiss them and

they kiss back. Our first kiss was perfect, but this one is better. We are so together it's like this is where I belong. On this cloud. This heart-shaped cloud.

Quella.

'Edi?' Archie pulls away from me. 'Your parents might come in.'

'They won't,' I tell him. 'They wouldn't interrupt while we're working.'

Archie shakes his head. 'We're *not* working,' he says.

'I know.' I want to kiss him again but he stands up.

'I better go,' he says.

I don't want him to go, but there doesn't seem much I can do about it. Besides, it's getting late. He gives me one more kiss. On the cheek this time.

When he's left, I try to take the kiss back to bed. I try to keep that feeling.

But it disappears.

I wish I could just cut it out of me, this loneliness.

I get under the covers and snuggle as though he's still here. I remind myself there will be more moments like the one we just had. Loads more.

It's all right, quella, I tell myself. *It's all right.*

I lie there for about half an hour before I remember I have to get up.

It's bin night.

Seven

'Edi, you can't go to school like that,' Mum says the next morning. She doesn't raise her voice. Her words are slow and controlled.

'Mum, it's just eyeliner. Everyone wears eyeliner.' Dad walks into the kitchen and I sigh loudly. He will be on her side for sure.

'Why do you want to wear eyeliner, Edi?' he asks.

'Because it looks pretty.' But I wish I hadn't even answered because I already know what he'll say next. It's not like I haven't heard it before.

'Being pretty is not an achievement,' he says.

Being a tool is, though. It's a giant achievement.

This is the bit where Dad pauses for effect. The lecture will continue in 5, 4, 3, 2, 1 …

'Working hard and using your intelligence and your natural talents, they are achievements,' he says, right on cue. Now Mum joins in. The two of them are a unit. As usual.

'You actually have to work harder for people to take you seriously when you're pretty,' she says.

I've been hearing stuff like this since I was little. Since people peered into my pram and made loads of exclamations about how beautiful I was.

I wish Mum and Dad would just stop saying it. If they bothered to get to know me, they'd know I realise being pretty isn't an achievement. I mean, it was quite nice being ranked number one on the hot list, but it didn't mean as much to me as it did to some of the other girls, like Limps, for instance. The thing is, I don't see anything wrong with wearing a tiny bit of eyeliner like I do on the weekends, even if it is against the school rules. I just want to look nice.

I don't care what Nelson and some random boys think. But I've got Archie now and I do care about that.

'Your mother and I have to go to work now. You'll take off the eyeliner before you go to school,' Dad says, as though it's settled.

I nod. There's no point arguing with my parents. I go to the bathroom and listen for the front door to close.

But I don't take off the eyeliner. I put on mascara as well.

I'm glad Hazel asks me to her place after school. I don't feel like going home. Mum and Dad will probably both be at work, but I text Mum and tell her I'm going to Hazel's to do homework just to cover myself in case.

'Are you okay?' Hazel asks me as we get back to her place. 'You seem a bit off.' She's right. I've been a bit off all day.

'I've just had a shitty day,' I say. 'It started with Mum and Dad telling me off for make-up and it just went downhill from there.'

'Harsh,' Hazel says. 'You've barely got any on.'

I shrug. There's no real way to explain what happened with Mum and Dad this morning. If I told Hazel how Dad says being pretty is not an achievement, it would sound like I think I'm hot.

'They go on and on about breaking school rules,' I say. 'Like *everybody* doesn't do it.'

Hazel nods. She always wears eyeliner and mascara. In fact, I reckon she was one of the first girls to do it, probably because she has a cool older sister. Hazel's interesting like that. She's really low-key in some ways, but she was also the first one of us to get a boyfriend.

'Nobody even notices except for Mr Chin,' says Hazel. 'So, it's fine unless he spots you.'

'Anyway, why are the teachers allowed and we're not?' I say. 'Like Ms Jensen. She should be banned from wearing it.'

'Totally,' Hazel agrees. Ms Jensen wears foundation on her face and never takes it down to her neck, so it looks like she's wearing an orange mask all the time.

'Hi, girls.' We don't notice him at first because he's sort of buried in a beanbag, but it's Hazel's mum's boyfriend.

'Hi, Jason,' Hazel says. 'What are you doing? Where did that beanbag come from?' She gives me a sideways look as if to say, *check out what this dude comes up with.*

Jason flips his dreadlocks so they fall down the back of the beanbag. 'I brought it over from my place, Hazel. To balance the energy in here. You should always have an even number of seats in a lounge room. It's just basic feng shui.'

'Yeah, just basic,' Hazel says, pulling me out of the lounge room like she's rescuing me. I don't feel like I need rescuing, though. I think it's nice of him to try to balance the energy, even if it's a tiny bit freaky. I wish I could get him over to my place to balance the energy there.

We go into the kitchen. There are heaps of dishes in the sink. At our place, nothing is left out. Everything is put away in its own spot. Bowls, plates, cups, all separated. Like we are.

'So, what else happened to make your day shitty?' Hazel asks as we walk back to her room with hot chocolates. Before I can answer, her phone beeps.

'Check this out,' she says with a giggle. On the screen, there's a photo of Leo. It looks like he's in a changing room in a clothes shop. He's wearing a shirt and tie, and has a really kooky look on his face. 'He's shopping with his mum,' Hazel explains. 'She's making him wear a collar and tie to some wedding they're going to.'

Hazel sits on her bed and leans against the headboard to text back. I sit on the end of the bed feeling weird. The way she's always in touch with Leo highlights why my day went from bad to worse.

'How do you do that, Haze?' I ask.

'What?'

'Like, how do you get Leo to, I don't know, hang with you? Talk with you and stuff?'

'Like, how did I *train* him?' Hazel asks with a giggle.

'Exactly,' I say. It's good, talking to Hazel. Out of all the caravan crew, she's the one who gets things the most. I have to spell everything out with Jess. And Limps always *thinks* she gets me when she actually doesn't half the time.

'That's just how it happens with Leo and me,' Hazel says. 'It's a bit different with Archie, I guess. Like, Leo's not into sports so he has more time.'

'Archie is obsessed,' I say and lie back on the bed. 'I

barely even spotted him today. He played soccer all lunch time. Again.'

Hazel nods. 'He really likes you, though, Edi,' she says. 'Leo reckons he talks about you heaps.'

'Ooh, what does he say?'

'He says ... you're the hottest girl he's ever met.'

Being pretty is not an achievement. 'What else?' I ask.

'Um ... that you're the hottest girl he's ever met?' she says again and we both laugh. But I want more than that. If he knew me better, if we had more time together, I know there would be more between us.

I just have to make it happen.

'So, you know how Jess and Cam have been flirting all week?' Hazel says, changing the subject.

'Yeah,' I say, though, to be honest, I haven't really noticed.

'Jess says that Cam reckons ...'

I nod as Hazel goes on, but I'm not really with her. *There has to be a way to get to spend some more time with Archie,* I think. *He's obviously not going to make time for me at school because of stupid soccer, but ...*

'She reckons she's got heaps to talk about when we all get together on Friday. I think Olympia has some stuff going on too. You still good for the caravan meeting?'

You can come for a cooking lesson anytime, Edi.

'Yep. Sure,' I say. I feel better. Lots better, actually.

Because I've just thought of a way to spend more time with Archie.

Eight

You come for a cooking lesson anytime, Edi.

You come for a cooking lesson anytime, Edi.

I chant it inside my head as I walk over to Archie's on Thursday afternoon. All I'm doing is taking Archie's mum up on her offer. And if Archie is there, that will be a bonus.

I resend the text message I sent to Mum yesterday about doing homework at Hazel's house. She probably won't even notice it's exactly the same one. I'm almost getting used to lying all the time, but I feel a little pang about it as my phone makes the little *message sent* sound.

It's not like I have any other choice, though. Today was even worse than usual. Archie didn't have soccer training for once, so we ate lunch together. But then Eliza came over to where we were sitting on the slope and said Archie had to go to the library with her to do some work on their project. And he went. That really sucked.

As I walk up Archie's driveway, I think about turning back. What if Archie's mum doesn't even remember making the offer? That would make me look totally weird.

I see her through the kitchen window. No turning back now. I take a deep breath and walk to the front door. She's opened it before I even get there.

'Hello, love,' she says. She does look surprised to see me, but not *bad* surprised. 'Archie is over at his cousin Rio's *awful* new flat.' She pauses, as though considering the state of Rio's flat. I gather this is the cousin who Archie was helping to move out after we met at the skate park. His mum doesn't seem very happy with the shift.

'He shouldn't be much longer. No food over there! Come in.' She walks down the hallway and I follow. 'You can wait here while I make dinner. It will be nice to have some girl company,' she says and the way she says it makes me feel better.

'Actually,' I say as we reach the kitchen, 'I was ... I was wondering if I could have that cooking lesson?'

'Ah, of course you can,' she says and she really does look pleased. It makes me relax.

'Today I am making – *we* are making – pesto for pasta. It's Archie's favourite. He loves it so much he could eat it every night.'

It's nice, being in the de Souza family kitchen, even though it's a little weird that Archie's not there. I wash basil leaves and then Archie's mum shows me how to sprinkle salt over the garlic to make it easier to crush. I'm enjoying it so much that I almost forget about Archie. We're up to toasting the pine nuts when I hear the front door open.

My heart thumps. The pine nuts sizzle. I forget to move them around the frying pan and Archie's mum rescues them from burning by taking the pan off the flame.

I wish she could rescue me.

'Mum! Rio bought the best PlayStation game! We've just been playing it and he's let me borrow it for the night.'

Archie's voice flies down the hallway. 'He ordered it over the net and I so want it. I promise I will wash your car.' There's a pause as though Archie is considering something as he walks towards the kitchen. 'I'll wash Dad's too,' he adds and his mum smiles at me and shakes her head.

'He never does it properly, he always misses spots,' she whispers, like it's a secret just between the two of us. I try to smile back but I feel my lips wobble at the edges.

I hope he's happy to see me.

'I can put in half,' Archie's voice is closer now and it's kind of funny how he's negotiating with his mum even though she hasn't said anything. 'Or two-thirds if you … Edi! What are you doing here?'

His eyebrows lock together and his head jerks backwards, like he's shocked.

I try to steady my heart.

Shocked doesn't mean unhappy. Shocked doesn't mean unhappy …

'Archie, *gentile*,' Archie's mum says and she speaks Italian to him so I don't get exactly what's going on but I think it's something to do with him being rude.

'Sorry, Edi,' he says. 'I just … it's just … I didn't expect … a bit of a surprise.' He toys with the PlayStation disc in his hand.

I breathe deeply and try to sound calm. 'Your mum offered to give me a cooking lesson,' I say.

He nods. I *think* he's okay.

'So, Edi,' says Archie's mum, as if there's nothing awkward going on. 'After that, all you have to do is put everything into a blender with a bit of olive oil and you're done. You have all that?'

'Yes. Thanks,' I say. I pick up a dishcloth and I turn away from Archie and I'm about to wipe the bench like I would if I was cooking at home, but my hand is trembling. I can feel Archie's eyes on me and I really don't know if he's okay with me being here.

Archie's mum shakes her head like I shouldn't even think of helping her tidy up and takes the dishcloth from me. Then she goes to the fridge, gets out a plate of chopped fruit, hands it to Archie and shoos us out of the kitchen.

I follow Archie into the lounge room, even though I'm really nervous about what he might say.

I sit on the couch. Archie doesn't say anything. He walks straight over to the PlayStation and puts the disc in.

'I hope you don't mind that I came over,' I say to his back.

Archie shrugs his shoulders. It's not the reaction I was looking for.

The TV screen goes on and the PlayStation game loads. Archie walks back to the couch with the remote. He doesn't sit very close to me.

'It's okay,' he says. He presses play, which is really annoying. There's a space-age warrior on screen. Archie makes him jump and run and collect points.

'It's just …' I say and then stop.

Archie click, clicks. Every time he wins points, there's loud music. I just sit there, feeling awkward.

'Can you pause it?' I ask.

Archie hits the pause button. Then he turns to me. 'Anything else?' he asks, and the way he says it brings a sting to my eyes. I blink and swallow. I feel like we're in a fight and I don't know how we got here.

'It's just … we don't really spend much time together, do we? You know, like Leo and Hazel?' My voice is wobbly.

Archie puts down the remote and shifts closer to me. It's such a relief when he does that I have to bite my lip. I so don't want to cry.

'Like at school, you mean, Edi?' His tone is softer. 'At lunchtime?' I think he feels bad for snapping at me before.

'Yeah, partly,' I say.

'That's because I play soccer. Leo doesn't,' Archie says and I can see him reaching for the remote like that explains everything and now he can go back to the game. But I really want him to understand, so I continue.

'The thing is,' I say, 'maybe it would be a bit easier to get some time together if you didn't play so much soccer,' I say.

'Oh,' Archie says. 'You don't want me to play soccer at lunchtimes?'

'No, I don't mean that,' I say quickly. 'Just *some* of the time, so we can hang out together. If you want to, I mean.'

'So you just want to hang out together a bit more, like Leo hangs out with Hazel, hey?' he asks.

'Yeah.'

'Okay,' he says and then he gets the cutest cheeky look

on his face. 'Leo's not going to beat me.'

I shake my head and roll my eyes but I'm smiling. 'It's not a competition,' I say and next thing I know Archie is tickling me and now I'm really laughing and I'm glad I came over, and I'm glad I said what I said. I think things are going to be even better between us from now on.

'I can't wait until the caravan meeting tonight,' Jess whispers to me. 'I've got so much to tell you all.'

I lean in as close to her as I can with Archie holding my left hand. We're sitting on the slopes at lunchtime, with Hazel, Leo and Olympia sitting behind us. It's a sunny day, not too hot and not too cold. No Eliza. Perfect!

'Oooh,' Archie says, raising my hand in the air. 'Good save, Pezza.' The soccer field is past the basketball courts, but he can obviously still make out what's going on. I don't mind.

There's a tap on my shoulder and I turn around. When I do, Archie lets go of my hand.

It's Olympia who tapped me. 'I have some special news too,' she says.

'Oh good,' I say, but Archie's hand is out of reach now. Because of her. And he's completely engrossed in that soccer game again.

'Edi, let's go shopping together and get stuff to make nachos,' she says. 'I have a feeling it's going to be a long meeting,' she says with a smile. 'We'll need sustenance.'

'Yeah, okay,' I reply. Mum and Dad are going to be out at some gala or something so it will be easy to use the kitchen without anyone breathing down our necks.

'It's actually okay sitting here,' Archie says. I reach for his hand again and squeeze it. 'You can really see the mistakes people are making. Like, Pezza should have passed to Nelson on that last …'

I squeeze his hand again, a bit harder.

'Sorry. I mean it's nice to sit with you, of course.' He laughs, then lets go of my hand and puts his arm around my shoulder.

I lean into him. I wish lunchtime could go forever.

'What are you up to on the weekend?' I ask.

'Er, I've got a bit on,' he says. 'Like Saturday and Sunday are chockers with soccer stuff and family stuff.'

That means I won't get to see him till Monday. Unless … 'What about tonight?' I ask.

Jess gives me a look.

'Nothing on tonight,' Archie says. 'Wanna hang out?' He obviously hasn't heard what Jess and Olympia have said about the caravan meeting. Lucky.

Archie has nothing on tonight. My parents are going to be out. We could be alone.

Jess's look turns into a glare. Olympia prods the base of my back with her foot.

I could go shopping and get stuff to make pesto. His favourite. He could eat it every night.

'Why don't you come over to my place?' I say, ignoring the foot that's now firmly implanted in my back. 'Say, six?'

'Cool,' Archie says.

The bell goes and Archie and Leo go together to their lockers.

'What about our caravan meeting?' Hazel says as we walk up the breezeway towards our lockers.

'I've been saving up all this stuff to tell you,' Jess adds and she's practically stomping. Olympia doesn't say anything for a while. When she opens her mouth, I expect she'll defend me.

'I have something I want to talk about too,' she says quietly.

I sigh. 'Come on, guys,' I say. 'Don't guilt me.' They're all being a bit OTT. It's only a caravan meeting after all. 'I had to do it. Archie and I have a chance to have the house to ourselves.'

Hazel shakes her head. 'You guys can come over to my place,' she says to Jess and Olympia.

'There, that's settled then,' I say.

'Yeah, I guess it is,' Olympia says.

The three of them walk in front of me as if they're annoyed.

Oh well, it's no biggie. They'll get over it. And I've got a whole night with Archie to look forward to!

Nine

I'm so running late. For starters, I forgot to get pine nuts at the supermarket and I had to go back and stand in the queue all over again.

As I walk home, I text Mum.

Okay if Archie comes over tonite? Have maths test on Monday.

Actually, that's true. Archie is coming over and I do have a maths test on Monday. I get the text back straight away, which is good because my phone is nearly dead.

That's impressive, Edi. V dedicated. Okay.

It was pretty smart to tell them Archie's tutoring me. It's definitely making things easy.

I rush home. Mum and Dad have already left. I stick my phone on the charger in my bedroom and go down to the kitchen. I put my iPod in the docking station, turn up my music really loud like I can never do when Mum and Dad are home, and start on the pesto.

It's nice having the house all to myself, and knowing that Archie's going to be here soon. I sing along to the music as I cook. The pesto looks okay. It's not as green as Mrs de Souza's. I'll have to ask her about that next time I see her. I have a packet of gnocchi I bought from the supermarket. It's not homemade, but I think it will be fine. I set the table so I won't have much to do when Archie gets here. When it's set, I stand back and look at it.

Soon, Archie will be sitting across the table from me. I'm going to ask about stuff. Stuff other than soccer. It will be good to find out what his favourite music is. I could even talk to him about PlayStation games. There's a couple I like. Maybe he'll like Guitar Hero too? I'll tell him about my brother – how he lives in New York and he's smart and funny. How he works really hard but he still finds time to Facebook and even Skype sometimes, though the time difference is a killer. So he'll know more about me too. About what I'm like on the inside.

Then, after dinner, we'll go into the caravan. Like we did last time, but this time it won't be rushed. We'll have some time in there. Together. I feel soft just thinking about it. All warm and melty.

He's going to be here in fifteen minutes, and I haven't even changed out of my school uniform yet.

I float upstairs to my bedroom. I think I'll wear my yellow top. I lay it out on my bed with my pale blue jeans. I can still hear my music and I'm kind of dancing, swaying even, as I get dressed. When that's done, I sit at my dressing table and brush my hair.

There's a text message on my phone. I pull it out of the charger and check it. It's from Archie.

Hey Edi. Soz but have family thing 2nite with the Gabriels so can't come to yours. x

I put the phone down. I pick it up again, hoping the message has changed somehow.

It hasn't.

I do it again.

It still hasn't.

I put my head on the dressing table. The warm, melty feeling I had before has turned hard and cold in my chest. My heart is ice.

A family thing 2nite with the Gabriels …

I'm pretty sure that's Alice's family. Her surname is Gabriel. They're old family friends of Archie's family.

When I finally lift my head up, it's heavy with thoughts that bump into each other.

I've made pesto. Specially.

The table is set.

The girls are at Hazel's without me.

I've got nothing.

If Archie couldn't come here, why doesn't he ask me to go to his?

The last thought stays with me as I go downstairs to the kitchen. Maybe I can put the pesto into a container and take all the stuff over to Archie's? He probably just hasn't thought of it. That's all. I text back.

How about I come to yours? I can bring stuff.

I stare at the kitchen table, the two table settings. And wait. It feels like ages before he texts me again.

Soz. Going to Alice's. Mum says rude to take an extra. Gtg. Call u soon xx

I am an 'extra'.

Alice is 'family'.

I am alone.

It's Friday night and everyone is doing something, except for me. Even Mum and Dad are out and they won't be home until nine o'clock. Two and a half hours from now.

I switch off the iPod. I don't feel like listening to music anymore. I sit down. Where I was going to sit opposite Archie. Which used to be opposite Jai.

I send the girls a group text.

Actually I might be able to come over after all. U there?

Ten minutes. Fifteen minutes. Nothing.

I ring Hazel's home number. Her mum answers. 'The girls went for pizza and to see a movie. I'd say they'd be in the movie by now,' she says.

I hang up. Jess said she had something to spill tonight. When it's Jess's turn, it's always funny. She goes off track and leads us through all these funny little stories, and we have to keep bringing her back to the point.

I remember, suddenly, that Olympia had something to share as well. The thought catches inside my chest. I should have at least asked her what it was today.

I put my head into my hands. They're probably all laughing. Sharing popcorn in the movie theatre. Or sharing stories afterwards. Life stories.

I'm here, all alone. Missing out. I'm missing out on the girls, on Archie, on *everything*.

I turn on the TV in the lounge room. There's nothing good on. TV noises waft around me. I get my laptop and go on Facebook, but there's no-one I want to talk to.

I stare out the window. There's a hollow space inside me. Tears slide down my cheeks. There's no-one to see them.

It's 7 p.m. here. Which means it would be 5 a.m. in New York. Jai would be asleep.

I don't care. I pick up my phone and dial. I imagine it

ringing into the early morning at my brother's flat, halfway around the world. Six times, seven times, eight times.

'Hello?' It's a blurry Jai voice. A sleepy Jai voice. 'Hello?'

'Jai,' I say, and as soon as I say his name aloud, I can't hold it in anymore. I just cry into the phone.

'Edi?' Jai says, as though he's really awake now. I feel bad because he's got to get up in a few hours and he's got so much on his plate and I can't even talk. All I can do is bawl. He's on the other side of the world and he'll think something is horribly wrong – and things *are* horribly wrong, but he might think someone has died and every time I think a new thought, I seem to cry harder.

'Edi? Edi, what's happened? Are you okay? Edi, take a breath. Talk to me.'

I try to breathe.

'Honey, what's wrong? What's going on?' Jai has never in my entire life called me honey. He sounds so panicked.

'Jai,' I say, my voice trembling, 'I'm okay. Mum and Dad are okay. I just …' I suck in a breath. Blow it out. 'I just miss you!' I say and I feel like a complete idiot because we know we love each other but I don't talk like this to my brother, and I definitely don't call him in the early morning and send him into a panic.

'Edi, calm down.' I can just about see Jai on the other end of the phone, trying to figure out what to do with his crazy sister.

'I miss you too,' Jai says. 'Of course I do. But is something wrong? Are you hurt?'

'No. I'm fine,' I say and the crying has calmed down and I just feel like an idiot for getting him out of bed. It was so stupid of me to call.

'I'm just … I'm just tired. Honestly, I'm fine,' I say. 'Go back to bed.'

When I get off the phone, I just sit there. I'm still staring out the window when a taxi pulls into our driveway. Mum and Dad get out and I wipe my eyes. It's weird they got a taxi. Mum normally drives. She must have left her car at the gala. When they come in, I think I know why they've left the car. Mum's a bit wobbly on her feet. It looks like she's had one too many champagnes.

'Hi, honey,' she says, coming over to the couch. 'Has Archie gone already?'

I shake my head. Try to sound fine. 'It ended up that he couldn't make it,' I say.

Mum sits next to me on the couch while Dad goes into the kitchen. She looks at me. She doesn't say anything for a while. Then she reaches out and tucks some stray hair behind my ear. She hasn't done anything like that for ages. It makes the lump in my throat grow bigger.

'Oh, Edi,' she says. 'He seems like a nice boy. I'm … um …' she stops there and I think that's it, but finally, as Dad comes into the lounge, she continues. 'I'm sure there's a good reason why he couldn't come.'

Now there's a fluttery feeling inside my chest to add to the lump in my throat. Could it be that she knows?

'Of course there's a reason, Alisha,' Dad says, standing behind the couch and opening the window. 'We'll have to pay him. Tutors don't work for free. Let's get onto that during the week.'

There's a little frown on Mum's face and she tilts her head to the side. She's still looking at me. It's kind of intense.

'Edi's not a baby anymore. How about we let her figure

that out,' she says, and she doesn't say it like a question. It's like, for once, she's not waiting for Dad to agree with her. Dad comes around to the front of the couch. He looks confused.

'You're not making any sense, Alisha,' he says. He starts walking towards their bedroom. 'Come on, we'd better get some sleep. Edi, I'll help you with your maths tomorrow.'

I roll my eyes. Dad did the maths level I'm at about a hundred years ago. He doesn't seem to get that everyone uses different methods now.

Mum gets up from the couch. I can't believe it, but she's actually rolling her eyes too. Just a little bit.

'Edi. The sun'll come out tomorrow,' she says, and suddenly I want to cry all over again, because I'd almost forgotten. When I was little we used to watch *Annie* together all the time, and it drove Jai and Dad mental. I actually wish, for once, that Mum would stay up with me for a while. I don't ask her to, though. It's probably better if she just goes to bed. I could end up spilling everything. And regretting it.

'Night, Mum,' I say.

She walks down the hallway behind Dad.

When she's halfway down the hall she stops, then turns around and says, just loud enough for me to hear, 'Bet your bottom dollar that tomorrow, there'll be sun.'

Ten

The sun does come up the next morning. It seeps through the gaps in my blinds when Jai calls at 7 a.m. The phone call is only quick because he's in between classes. He just wants to check how I am. I think he's pretty confused when I tell him I really am okay and that he's not allowed to tell Mum and Dad I called, but he seems relieved too. It's nice to know he cares. I go back to sleep afterwards.

At nine o'clock there's a knock at my bedroom door.

'Go away,' I say, but the door swings open and Dad's standing there.

'Come on, Edi. Rise and shine. I've got two hours before I have to go into work. Let's get onto that maths revision since your tutor didn't show last night.'

I groan. There's no point protesting. I'll be doing maths with my muesli.

He gives me five minutes to organise myself. We sit at the kitchen table with my books. It's actually not as bad as I thought it would be. Dad has a different way of getting to the answers than Mr C has taught us, but I kind of get it. In fact by the end, I feel like I'll probably do okay in the test on Monday. Finally, he checks his watch and gets up from the table.

'Thanks, Dad,' I say. He hasn't said anything about it but he normally plays golf on Saturday mornings. I'm pretty sure he cancelled so he could do this with me, and it makes me feel a bit bad. Now he'll be going straight from this to work. It's not much of a Saturday, really.

'You're welcome, Edi,' Dad says. He goes to get his car keys out of the tray and turns back, like he's deciding whether to say something or not. 'You're a clever girl, you know.'

It comes out sounding small and he's out the door before I can say anything back, but it's funny how it seems to nuzzle into my heart. From Dad, that's the ultimate compliment.

The sun really has come up. I feel pretty good. Archie will call today and things will be totally back on track.

Mum's out, but she's left me a list of things to get at the supermarket. I check my phone in the cereal aisle. Nothing. I check my phone in the toiletries aisle. Nothing. I check my phone in the queue. Nothing.

That's the way it is all day. I'm still checking my phone just before I go to bed.

Nothing. Zip. I check out his last text. *Call u soon.*

When is soon?

I have a haircut booked for Sunday. Just a wash and a trim. I have my phone in my hand as Audrey shampoos my hair.

Archie might have run out of credit, or forgotten that he was supposed to call me?

Audrey lifts my hair into one giant, shampooed spike.

'Can you wait for a sec?' I say. I have an idea. I'll take a photo of me like this on my phone and send it to him. It will be funny, not heavy. Like Leo's photo from the change room. Hazel and Leo do it all the time – communicate.

Audrey takes a pic for me. I look like an alien. It's perfect. I add a bit of text at the bottom. *Call me x.*

Audrey is doing the trim when my phone beeps.

It's so cute. It's a photo of Archie on the soccer field, smiling and kicking the ball up to his own hands. Pezza is behind him, making rabbit ears. One of the other players must have taken it.

I hold it out in front of me and stare at it, keeping my head straight so that Audrey can do the trim.

I must have stared at it for too long. 'Oh my god, Audrey,' I moan. 'You've cut it too short!'

Audrey looks at me in the mirror. 'It's great,' she says. 'And anyway, we got rid of all the split ends.'

My photo staring has cost me about five centimetres of hair. Plus, there's no text underneath saying when he's going to call. But I don't care. At least he sent it, and he was smiling, which means everything is all right.

If he hasn't called by five, I'll call him. No big deal.

V

It's ten past five when I go into the caravan to make the call. His phone rings.

Brr, brr.

I'm just going to be bright and cruisy. I'll ask him how his soccer game went today. I'll ask him how his family dinner went on Friday night. I'll tell him about my haircut from hell …

Brr, brr.

'Hello? Is that you, Edi?'

It's not Archie's voice. It's a girl's voice. My heart thumps. *Eliza.*

'Why are *you* answering Archie's phone?' It just jumps out of my mouth.

'Oh, it *is* you, Edi,' Eliza says breezily. 'Archie's not here right now. He's just gone to get us a snack and we're pretty busy actually, so now might not be a very good time …'

'What are you doing there?'

'Oh, per-lease,' Eliza says, 'take a chill pill. We're doing our *project*.' The way she says project is so annoying. It's all soft and sexy, like they're on a date or something.

'Who is it, Eliza?' It's Archie's voice in the background. The next bit is muffled, like someone's placed their hand over the receiver. And, honestly, it's at least a minute before he comes to the phone. It feels like they're discussing me. By the time he takes the phone, I'm furious.

I remember when I did the dare at Archie's party and sat on his knee for a whole round of truth or dare. How Eliza said at the top of her voice, *That round is over, Edi. You can get off Archie's lap now.* If she hadn't said that, who knows what might have happened? Maybe Archie and I would've started going out together that night, and we'd really *get* each other by now. None of this stuff would even be happening.

'Edi?' Archie says. 'I was going to call you.'

'When?'

'Oh … um … soon,' he says. 'I've just been pretty busy and …'

'Yeah, doing your *project*.' I say it like Eliza just said it and as soon as it comes out of my mouth, I wish I could stick it back in.

'Oh my god, Archie,' I can hear Eliza say, and it's hard to work out exactly what she says next, but it sounds like, 'Needy much? Needy Edi.'

'What did she say?' I demand.

'Nothing,' he lies. Then there's a hand over the receiver again and more muffled talking. My breathing is fast and shallow and it echoes over the phone line. It's ages before he comes back.

'Okay, Edi. I don't really get what's going on here, but Eliza's out of the room now.'

I try to calm myself. To slow my breathing.

'Archie, she's a –' I'm about to say exactly what I think of Eliza, but he cuts me off.

'Edi, do you think things are working out between us?' His tone is exactly the same as it was that time I asked him to pause the PlayStation and he snapped at me. But he got over that. Didn't he?

It's a punch in the chest. Archie might be delivering

those words, but they don't sound like his words at all. I bet they're *her* words. They wind me.

'Yes,' I say and I sound like a kitten mewing.

'Really?' he says. 'I'm not so sure.'

I don't like where this is heading. Not one bit. I need to cut it off. I need for the next bit not to happen. I need to be able to talk to him without her being around. Not just out of his room. Nowhere near him.

'Let's talk about this tomorrow. I have to go,' I say. 'Mum's calling me.'

I hang up my phone. Lie back on the bed, look up at the cloud picture.

It will be okay, I tell myself. Things just got a bit off track this weekend. I know we like each other. And I get on so well with his mum and dad.

I'm his *quella*.

When my phone beeps I don't look at it for a while. But then I wonder if it's Archie, wanting to apologise. I pick it up. Look at the screen.

I think we should cool it for a while, Edi. Sorry. Let's be friends.

All I want to do is lie there. And cry. But so far, there are no tears.

'Edi, dinner's ready.' Mum's at the caravan door. She walks in and sits on the bed. 'Edi, are you all right?' she asks.

I breathe out. Just when I need some space, there she is. 'Yep,' I say quickly. It's not like Mum would get it.

'Sweetheart,' she says. It's really awkward because she doesn't say stuff like that and it sounds really forced. I don't want the tears to come in front of her. We just don't do that stuff in my family.

'Sweetheart,' she repeats, 'I know something's going on with you.' She pats my knee stiffly, like I'm a pet. I think about Archie's mum after his soccer match, squeezing his cheeks together and kissing both sides. Completely natural. 'Archie is your boyfriend, right?' She says it like she's solved a crossword puzzle. Like she's got the answers when really she knows *nothing*.

'Actually, no. No, he isn't.' It comes out more harshly than I meant it to sound.

Mum gets up. That's all she has. 'Okay, come in for dinner, then,' she says.

V

It's really late, but I send a group text to Hazel, Jess and Limps from my room after dinner. Just so they know. Just so someone knows how I feel.

Then I think about how I ditched them on Friday night, and hope they still care.

And that's when, finally, I find my tears.

Eleven

They're all waiting for me at the school gates on Monday morning. Hazel. Jess. Limps.

'Are you okay?' Olympia hugs me.

'What a dog act,' Jess says. 'Breaking up with you by text. Like, some guys do it on Facebook and that's even worse. I know a guy who just changed his status to single and that's how the girl knew they weren't together anymore. Well, I actually don't know the guy but I ... hey, your haircut is awesome, Edi. It's very Cleopatra. Where did you ...'

'Edi,' Hazel interrupts Jess. 'Seriously, are you all right?'

I nod. It's only a small nod because I'm not sure if I am all right.

'We're going to stick with you as much as we can today, Edi,' Hazel continues. 'I think it's probably best if we try to avoid Archie. If you see him, just pretend you don't.'

'Yep,' Olympia says. 'That's the plan. Plus, we all just went in and asked Pip if we can use the drama room at lunchtime to practise that skit we've been working on.'

'Pip said yes,' Hazel adds, 'though I don't think she really believed us about the practice.'

'Yeah, well, we don't really need to practise, cos we know it already,' says Jess, 'Which means we can have an emergency meeting and no-one else will be around, so it can be private. We can figure out what to do and then you'll feel better.'

'So you just have to make it until lunchtime, Edi,' Limps says and she's standing close to me and checking out who's coming through the school gates like she's my bodyguard or something.

You'd think I would have used up all my tears last

night, but there's a prickling in my eyes that feels dangerous. They're treating my broken heart as an emergency. I'm not sure I deserve it.

The first bell goes. Hazel and Jess walk in front of me and Limps walks behind.

It's almost like being carried.

I work really hard all morning. The sort of hard work that blocks out everything else. I'm pretty sure I ace the maths test. I put so much into my English comprehension questions that they're twice the length of anyone else's.

At recess, Jess and I walk to the library. People talk behind their hands as I pass them and it's awful. I suppose everyone knows he's broken up with me. News travels fast at our school. I try not to pay attention, but a girl from our year whose name I don't even know yells out at me.

'Edi,' says Anya, or Angela, or whoever she is. I brace myself for whatever's coming. '*I* really like your haircut. You look awesome.'

'Thanks,' I say quietly. Now I wonder whether the rumour is that Archie has broken up with me because of my new haircut, when he hasn't even seen it yet. I keep walking.

For once, I'm glad that Jess has a million things to say and even though I'm not really listening, at least it's something to distract me from the whispers.

I don't see Archie at all, thank god. I don't know if I'd be very good at ignoring him. The weirdest thing is that I do feel like I tried hard with him. But it didn't seem to do me any good. I must have done something wrong, even if I can't work out what it was.

School work is way easier than real life. At least most of it makes sense.

As soon as Limps and I walk into the drama room at lunchtime, something shifts inside me. It's like there's been a ton of bricks inside my chest all morning where my heart should be.

There's something about the drama room that makes me feel good. For starters, Pip has put up posters of theatre shows and movies all around the walls. There's Marilyn Monroe with her white dress blowing up, a huge smile on her face. There's James Dean looking moody and Zac Efron and Lindsay Lohan.

There are also loads of giant cushions on the floor instead of chairs and tables, so you can really get comfy. But the main reason I like this room is because of the classes we've had in here with Pip. We've done role plays where I can forget I'm Edi Rhineheart and become someone completely different.

I wish I could be someone else right now. But at least being here is soothing. At least here there's no danger of running into Archie.

'Edi,' Limps says, arranging four cushions into a circle. 'I reckon that Eliza made Archie break up with you.' She pauses, cushion to her chest, and looks right at me as though she's really sure of what she's saying. 'It's totally obvious that she's into him. Anyway, he'd be mad to like her. You're, like, ten times prettier.'

I sigh and flop onto a cushion. Limps makes it sound like her declaring I'm prettier than Eliza is kind of the end of it all, and nothing else really matters. She might be partly right about Eliza. I am pretty sure that she likes Archie, but I don't really think he likes her back. Not in that way. I feel like I'm missing something.

'You're better off without him,' Limps tries again.

I shrug. I don't feel like I'm better off without him. And, honestly, Limps hasn't even had a real boyfriend, so I don't think she understands.

The door slides open. I get a bit of a shock when I see that Alice is here with Hazel and Jess. I mean, she's great and everything, but she's not part of our inner circle, the caravan crew. It makes me bristle a bit, but then I look at Hazel. She's raising her eyebrows at me and tilting her head slightly towards Alice, just so I can see, and I think I know what's going on. Alice knows Archie as a friend. It kind of hurts to admit it to myself, but she probably knows him better than I do. Hazel must have brought her along in case she can explain things a bit.

Hazel sets a cushion next to me and motions for Alice

to sit there. I glance over at Limps. She's set her cushion down and she's crossing her arms and biting her lip. I can't tell if she's mad at Hazel for organising this, or mad at herself for not organising it.

Jess and Hazel sit across from us. When Alice sits, she pulls her school dress over her knees. It reaches right down to her ankles. Her school shoes are lace-ups, like the boys wear. One of them is untied. The rest of us have T-bars. I make a mental note to point that out to her some time, since she's asked me to tell her about fashion. Jess and Hazel start talking about something. I don't really listen.

'Sorry to hear about you and Archie,' Alice says. 'Hazel told me.'

'Oh, so Archie didn't tell you himself?' I ask.

'No, I haven't seen him since Friday night,' she replies. I feel disappointed. I was kind of hoping he would have told her why he broke up with me. But if she hasn't spoken to him since Friday, that seems unlikely.

'He broke up with me,' I say.

Alice nods, like she knows that too.

'I don't know why,' I say, and there must be something

weird about my voice because Jess and Hazel stop talking and look at me.

'I don't *really* know either,' Alice says, but there's something about the way she says *really* that makes me think she might know. Or that she might have figured it out, even if Archie didn't tell her himself. Maybe she's been able to spot something I haven't.

'I thought things were going well,' I say. 'Like, I got on really well with his parents.'

Alice nods slowly, like she's taking it all in. But there's a little frown on her forehead. 'Mmm, yep, I do remember him saying you had a cooking class with his mum,' she says softly.

'It's really cool how she taught you to make pesto,' Jess says. 'I like pesto. I had it one time at this restaurant, though, and they made it a really light green colour and honestly it looked like snot and … oops … sorry.'

I'm staring at the little furrow in Alice's brow. There's something she's not telling me.

'Was that okay with him?' I ask. It's weird that I still don't really know how he felt about that.

Alice shakes her head, as though she's deciding whether to tell me something. When she finally speaks, everyone's listening. 'I'm not sure it's the actual reason,' Alice says.

'Can you tell me anyway?' I ask. 'Please?'

Alice taps her foot. Then she ties her shoelace. Like she's still deciding whether to say whatever it is that she's thinking.

'Well,' Alice says slowly, 'this is just what I think, okay? Archie definitely thinks you're pretty. But he's kind of … well, maybe he's not sure that you guys have much in common. Much to actually talk about.'

'We haven't even had a chance to find out,' I blurt out. 'He's always playing soccer, talking about soccer, or breathing soccer! We would have got a chance if it wasn't for Eliza.'

Olympia unfolds her arms and throws her hands in the air. 'Yeah, it's totally Eliza who caused the problem,' she says. 'Obviously.'

'Leo reckons Eliza has liked Archie for ages, and he's not into her,' Hazel says.

'I don't think it has much to do with Eliza,' Alice offers.

'It's more … well, a combination of things. Archie was a bit surprised that you turned up to his house when he wasn't there. And he does like to play soccer at lunchtimes. I think, maybe … maybe it was all just a bit too full-on for him.'

I close my eyes. Alice's opinion sinks like a stone inside me. *Needy Edi.*

I see myself walking over to his place for a cooking lesson, convincing myself it would be okay. Feeling more at home there, with his parents, than I feel at my own house. Cancelling our caravan meeting for a dinner with Archie. Asking him not to play soccer at lunchtimes.

And it's all been for nothing.

Alice is right. I feel sick. No wonder he dumped me.

Twelve

I sit there quietly and I'm pretty sure the look on my face tells the others I don't want to talk about Archie anymore. Alice leaves so there's just the four of us again.

'So, Limps,' Hazel says. 'How did it go last night?'

Olympia throws her head back and groans.

'How did what go?' I ask, because I have no idea what they're talking about.

'Oh,' Jess intercepts the question, 'I keep forgetting you weren't there on Friday night, Edi.' She gives Limps a little smile with raised eyebrows, like she's getting permission to tell me what's going on with Olympia. 'Limp's mum and dad were going to have dinner together last night,' she says, and I already know pretty much what's going on.

Olympia's parents have split up, but sometimes they talk like they're going to get back together. The worst thing is, Olympia's mum tells her everything, and it's like strapping her into a rollercoaster ride because Limps really wants it to happen and it never actually does.

Limps shakes her head. It's awful that she directs her answer to Hazel and Jess. It reminds me I wasn't there for her on Friday night. I was too wrapped up in Archie.

'Well,' Olympia says, 'Mum got all dressed up. She left our place at seven-thirty.'

'Yeah,' Hazel says, 'and then what?'

'She was home by nine,' Olympia says. She says it sarcastically, like she doesn't care anymore, but I know she does. 'They didn't even make it to main course.'

'I'm so sorry, Limps,' I say, and I really mean it. I'm so sorry I wasn't there for her on Friday night. And I'm sorry that her parents keep doing this to her. It's not fair.

'It's okay, Edi,' Limps says, shoulders slumping. 'Like,

how many times? I'm an idiot to even go there in my mind. I just wish she wouldn't tell me. Like, I really need to know how he drinks too much? How he's not up-to-date with maintenance payments? And this is after she's gone all gooey and told me that she still loves him, that he's kind and funny and he's still the one for her.'

Limps is looking right at me, wide-eyed, like I can give her some answers. It hits me hard. Limps thinks of me as her absolute best friend. And even if she can be a bit of a shadow at times, and she seems to be all thingy about me getting closer to Hazel, she's always there for me. Always.

'You're not an idiot, Limps,' I say. I grab her hand because I really want to transmit this, and somehow it seems the part of me that's really sorry might be able to travel better this way. 'Your mum shouldn't tell you every little detail. She's your *mum*, not your bestie.'

As soon as I say that, I think of my own mum. She's definitely a mum, not a bestie. But maybe that's not all bad?

'That's the weird thing about getting older,' Hazel says thoughtfully. 'You find out your parents aren't perfect.'

Limps lays her head on my shoulder, and it seems she's

happy to listen to what Hazel's got to say from this angle.

'When Mum started going out with Jason, I just about lost it. I couldn't understand why she'd want to go out with him and it was partly because he was so dreadlocky and *spiritual*, but it was also partly because I thought Romy and I should be enough for her. But, the thing is …' She pauses and we all wait. 'The thing is, once she got around to telling me how lonely she'd been, I kind of had to adjust and it was a bit like a crash course in growing up. And now I can talk to her better than I ever did before Jason came along. About stuff. About Leo. You know what I mean?'

'My mum and I go for a milkshake after school once a week,' Jess adds. 'So we can catch up on things without the boys interrupting every five seconds. I get caramel usually, but sometimes I actually don't get a milkshake and I decide to get like an iced coffee cos they make them with cream and ice-cream and …'

Jess is off on one of her tangents. I'm not really listening to what she's saying, but there is something I can't avoid paying attention to.

Hazel talks to her mum about loads of stuff.

Jess has a regular time with her mum to talk.

Limp's mum tells her every little detail.

And my mum barely knows me.

'I can't talk to my mum about anything.' It just bursts out of me. Like the lid's been on this feeling forever and there's too much pressure behind it. 'All she and Dad care about is my grades. They don't even want to know about anything else.'

Everyone is quiet for a moment. Limps lifts her head off my shoulder.

'Have you *really* tried?' asks Jess. 'Like, my parents sometimes don't listen to me properly so I tell them to *focus* if I have something to say, and then they know that they have to pay attention.'

I have to admit, it's a pretty good question. Jess does that sometimes. You think she doesn't get it, but then she goes right to the heart of things.

'Well,' I say, but I don't say anything else. I'm thinking about Mum being all sweet when she came home on Friday night after Archie didn't turn up. I think about her asking me if Archie was my boyfriend. How I cut her off.

'I'm not sure.' What I *am* sure about, though, is these girls. How they're here for me even after I ditched them for Archie. How I love the way we share stuff, and how even just talking about my parents has made my heart feel lighter, and made me feel less lonely.

How I'm not going to make the mistake of ditching them again. If I ever get another boyfriend.

The door to the drama room slides open again. Pip looks in.

'How did you go, girls?' she asks. 'Did you get through everything?'

I look at her, then around at my little family of friends.

'Yep,' Olympia says quickly.

Pip gives me one of her looks. The quizzical one, eyes squinted, head to the side like she's trying to see inside me. I think of what she said to Dad at the parent–teacher interview about how I show emotional intelligence when I act. Remembering that makes me squirm under her gaze.

I haven't been showing any emotional intelligence with my friends. More like emotional *retardation*.

'It's good to get together and sort things out,' Pip says.

She could be talking about workshopping our skit, but I don't think so. Like I said, news travels at our school and it could have travelled into the staffroom. 'Sometimes things get complicated and you have to uncomplicate them,' she continues. 'It's always nice to have friends, Edi. To help put the pieces together.'

I look at Pip and smile. 'We didn't get through everything,' I say. 'But we did get through a lot.'

V

After dinner that night, Dad goes into his study to work. Mum sits on the couch in the lounge room. She puts on her old-lady glasses and opens her book. Normally, I'd go into my room or the caravan, and go on Facebook. But tonight I sit next to her on the couch. Well, not right next to her. Our couch is pretty big.

I can feel Mum glancing at me over the top of her glasses. She does it three times, going back to her book and then doing it again, like she's surprised I'm still here. Me too, I guess. It's not like I have something prepared to tell her. She's still looking down at her book when she speaks.

'I had a boyfriend when I was your age. His name was Alistair.'

'Really?' I say. I must sound surprised because I can see the corner of Mum's mouth twitching. Not a smile, but somewhere on the way to one.

'Mmm,' she says. 'He played the guitar. He wrote a song for me.' I. Can't. Believe. What. I'm. Hearing. I guess I presumed that Dad was Mum's first boyfriend.

'What was he like? What was the song like?' I feel like there are a lot of questions backing up behind these ones, but I don't want to spook her by asking too many. Mum puts down her book.

'He was sweet. The song was awful.'

I find myself edging closer. I know she's only said seven words, but the seven words are different. Those seven words open a door. Well, set a door ajar, maybe. I decide to tell her something.

'Archie broke up with me.'

Mum nods and she puts her book and glasses down on

the couch and looks at me. Properly. I can tell that she's already figured most of it out, without my help.

'I'm sorry, Edi,' she says. 'He seemed like a nice boy. And it was nice to have some …'

Mum pauses and I wait for her to continue, but it's like she's run out of steam. She just sits there.

'It was nice to have some boy energy in the house again?' I say it as a question. I'm not sure whether we're on the same wavelength. But I can tell we are when Mum nods.

'Yes, Edi. Exactly.'

We sit there together in silence and, to me, it's like we're both remembering the way it was when Jai was here. Like we can hear his loud voice, his stomping footsteps, his laughter.

'I miss Jai,' I say eventually.

'Me too.' says Mum. She puts her hand on top of mine. It's still a pet-type pat. But it's more than that. I can tell there's been a little connection between us. Just a tiny one. But that's something.

Thirteen

I don't see Archie at all the next day either. On Wednesday, I spot him. Well, I see his back once when he's walking down to the oval with his mates, but that's it. My heart lurches a bit when I see his back, his broad shoulders. But I'm okay.

It's cute how the girls change direction so I won't run into him. I can't help thinking about how much work I used to put into *accidentally* running into him before we started going out. It's weird that I'm trying to do the exact opposite now. Still, I'm happy to follow my friends.

After school, we all decide to go to the 7-Eleven for a slurpee. There's about a gazillion kids in the 7-Eleven when we get there because it's 7-Eleven's birthday and the slurpees are free.

'I'm going to start with cola, and then do raspberry and lime at the top,' Jess says.

'I'm having raspberry straight up,' Hazel says as we walk inside.

'I'm going to …' I look up mid-sentence.

Archie is there. By himself.

He sees me, and there's a flash of something over his face. There's a little smile and his hand goes up like he's about to wave.

My heart races. It thumps inside my chest. I'm angry with him because he hasn't really *tried* to get to know me and he broke up with me anyway, but I'm also remembering. Remembering his hand on the small of my back. His touch.

There's a little shake of his head and the smile is gone and his hand goes down.

I turn away from him. When I look back, he's gone.

'Oh my god,' Jess says. 'Are you okay, Edi?'

I nod. Try to slow my heartbeat. My hand shakes as I fill my cup.

'He looked …' Hazel says, touching my arm, 'he looked kind of sad, don't you think?'

'He was the one who broke up with Edi,' Olympia reminds us all. 'So he doesn't have the right to be sad.'

Jess and Olympia start to walk out with their giant drinks. Limps pauses to wait for me, but I wave them on and wait for Hazel.

'I still reckon he looked sad,' Hazel says softly.

'Come back to mine?' Hazel offers after 7-Eleven.

Jess and Limps both shake their heads. Their parents want them home. Mine won't be there for ages, so I say yes.

I make sure I say a proper goodbye to Jess and Limps, so Limps doesn't get all funny about me going to Hazel's. It seems to work. It doesn't take that much to make Limps feel more secure.

Hazel is texting Leo as the others walk off in the opposite direction. She seems kind of jumpy as we set off together. She keeps looking back behind her.

'What's up?' I ask as we reach her house. There's a bike on her front porch. It's old and rusty.

'That means Jason's here,' she says. She crosses her eyes and points to the bike. I have a feeling that she's avoiding my question. I know why in thirty seconds when I see Leo walking up the steps to the porch. And with him … *with him* … is Archie.

I gulp. Then I reach out and give Hazel a very hard pinch on the arm. She ignores it.

'Haze,' Leo says. 'I have to talk to you, urgently. Um … er, about this thing.'

I'm frozen. I think I'm staring. Archie is walking behind Leo as though he's hiding. Then Leo grabs Hazel's arm, almost exactly where I pinched her, and the two of them go inside.

I'm left on the porch with Archie and the bike. I don't know which one of us is the most rusty. When Archie speaks, it comes out in spurts, like his vocal cords haven't been switched on for a long time.

'Ah, hi … Edi … I … I … wanted to … you know … talk …'

There's a little bit of armour around my heart. I want to keep it there.

I half-sit against the windowsill, like it's no big deal.

Then Archie's mobile rings. He looks at the screen and mouths, *Mum*. Then he puts a finger up. 'One minute. Please?' he says.

I shrug again. I don't know if I'll wait. I'm not sure I want to hear what he has to say.

'Mum, we're not going to take over his dinner. Rio has food of his own.' There's a pause and I can hear his mum's voice coming over really loudly though I can't actually make out what she's saying.

'No, we can't just drop in there tonight. He might have people over.'

Archie's mum.

'Well, I guess he's not really comparing it to our house, Mum. I think he just needs to do his own thing.'

Archie's mum.

'Yeah, I promise. *Ciao.*' He looks at me and shakes his head and closes his eyes like he's trying to block out his mum talking. 'You too,' he says finally. Archie hangs up and throws both arms in the air.

'Mum's been mental about Rio moving out,' he says and he just half-sits next to me on the windowsill. 'He's my cousin, but he lived with us for three years. So now, he's moved to his own flat with some mates and it's like … it's like Mum can't handle it. She's still cooking the same amount as she did when he was living with us. But guess who has to eat it all?' Archie points to himself, and then continues.

It's sort of mesmerising. I've never seen him like this before. So far, he's been speaking to the air, but then he turns to me. 'Honestly, Edi, she really has to get over it. Or I'll be about thirty kilos heavier. Like, we *all* miss him, you know? I mean, he's been at our place since I was eleven. It's like, everywhere I look, there's Rio *not* being there.'

I feel my armour melting away. I mean, yes, part of me is thinking that Archie is still totally hot. But there's something else, something more. And I know we're not going through exactly the same thing. Like, Archie's mum sort of seems to overcompensate for Rio not being there, while my parents seem to *under*compensate. Archie's parents give him too much attention, and mine barely give me any.

Still, we're both missing people. That much is clear.

'I know what you mean,' I say softly. 'I have an older brother. He moved out last year. Not just away, but *away* away, to New York. It's like everywhere I look, Jai is not being there too.'

Archie's flecked green eyes look into my dark ones. Like he's seeing me differently too. He turns his whole body towards me and moves closer, but not like he's going to touch me. Like he wants to know more.

I think of how I felt in the caravan with Archie after he came over for dinner after training last Tuesday. I think of him holding me, and I remember feeling like we didn't need to talk. I'm not sure about that anymore. It's good, finding out something like this about each other. It makes me wonder what else there might be to discover.

'When I was at primary school,' I say, and I can tell

Archie is really listening by the way a little frown comes across his forehead as he concentrates. 'I used to pretend to forget my lunch. I'd take my real lunch in a bag, and leave my lunchbox at home. Then I'd get the school to ring home so Jai would bring it to school for me. I wanted everyone to see how cool my brother was.'

Archie's smile is gorgeous. 'Rio taught me ten soccer tricks in ten days once,' he says. 'But when I could do them better than him, he went crazy.' He makes a furious face and waves his hands in the air like he's miming Rio going crazy.

It's my turn to grin. 'One time Jai actually thought to open the lunchbox and saw it was empty. He still brought it up to the school, but told me I had to stop crying wolf.' I haven't thought of the next bit for aeons, but now it comes back to me. 'Then, right there in the playground, in front of everyone, he started howling like a wolf.' I start laughing with the memory of Jai howling in the playground. The other kids had no clue what was going on with my crazy brother. I was really embarrassed at the time, but now it just seems really funny. Plus, I never did that thing with the lunch again.

'Ah, a practical joker,' Archie says with a grin. 'Rio used a prankster app on my iPhone and called Mr Cartwright without blocking my number. He called me back fifteen minutes later and I answered. Sprung. I got a detention.'

'Oh my god, which app?' I ask.

'Hello, is that the pizza man?' Archie says in a kiddie voice. I know that app. The girls and I have used it heaps. It's hilarious. But it wouldn't have been hilarious to be sprung by Mr C.

'Obviously, they're both lunatics. Why would we miss them?' I say.

We're both laughing when Hazel and Leo step back out onto the porch.

'We've finished talking about … the thing,' Leo says.

I can feel Archie slide a little closer to me. The gap between us is electric. 'I think there's another … um … thing you need to talk about,' he says. 'Five minutes?'

Hazel gives a very small, hidden thumbs up as she goes back inside. Archie steps out from the windowsill so that he's in front of me. So we're face to face.

'Edi,' he says, serious now. 'Things didn't go … well … the way I wanted them to. I actually …' his voice trails off before he finishes his sentence, but I understand anyway.

'Why did we break up?' I ask.

He shakes his head. 'That's hard to … um … explain,' he says.

I wait, this time. I want him to *communicate* with me. I want us to communicate with each other.

'I got … a bit … well, freaked that you didn't want me to play soccer at lunchtime, because I really love soccer.'

'I know you do,' I say and nod. To let him know that I get it. That maybe, I *was* a bit too full-on.

He pauses. Then he breathes out and breathes in again like he's trying to suck in some words and it's really awkward, but he *is* seriously cute. He even rocks his school uniform.

'That's not all, I guess,' he continues. 'It's like we didn't really seem to have much to talk about. At least, that's what I *thought,*' he says softly, 'but after we broke up I kind of realised I hadn't given it much of a go.' He does stop talking this time.

'We only really talked about soccer,' I say, and there's something about saying it aloud that makes me feel giggly all over again.

'Jeez,' he says, like he's just realised something. 'You don't like soccer, do you, Edi Rhineheart?'

I think for a moment. Part of me just wants to tell him that of course I like soccer. Part of me doesn't want to lose that connection. But it's not a *real* connection. And now, after we've been able to talk about my brother and his cousin, I feel like we might be able to throw out the stuff that isn't real.

I want him to like me for me.

'Nup!' I say and it flies out of my mouth and the next thing I know, Archie has stepped forward and he has his hands around my waist and he's tickling me like he's never going to stop.

When he finally does, I take a step back away from him. I look him right in those gorgeous green eyes. My heart starts thumping in my chest.

I'm going to do it.

It's just like Hazel said. I'm ready. I don't *want* to wait around, hoping for him to ask me again. Not even five minutes. It feels like a waste of time.

We have so much to learn about each other, but at least we've made a start, and it's a way better start than last time. If for some freaky reason I've misjudged things and Archie just wants to be my friend, I'll be devastated. But I don't feel like I'm guessing about him liking me anymore.

The curtain on the window shifts a little and I see Hazel's face peek through. She gives me a little wave and I lift my hand in answer, so she knows I'm okay and the curtain falls back into place.

I have the best friends on the planet. If Archie says no, I'll live. I'm pretty sure of that.

'Archie?' My voice is a bit squeaky but I make myself go on. 'Do you want to try again? Do you want to go out with me?'

For a second, he doesn't react. There's nothing there. I can't read his eyes or his mouth. Zip. He blinks.

Then his whole face lights up. Eyes. Mouth. He gives me the lot, Archie de Souza.

'Yes.' He says it simply, and words aren't the easiest thing for Archie, but the way he pulls me into him? That's easy.

'Edi,' he says. I look up to him. 'I don't really want to pretend to be your maths tutor with your parents,' he says. 'It just doesn't feel very … honest, you know?'

I do know. I want to start again. It was unfair of me to ask him to act like he was something he's not. I don't want to pretend about anything anymore. I nod. 'Deal,' I say.

It's not going to be easy, being honest about Archie with Mum and Dad. At least Mum kind of gets some of what's going on. Even though she thinks I've broken up with Archie, at least she knows I've had a boyfriend. I hope she'll help me tell Dad. That will be something else entirely. Still, I have to try. It's the only way anything will change between us. I will try.

'Okay, time's totally UP,' Hazel says, stomping onto the porch with Leo following her.

Archie and I smile at them.

Hazel gives us the thumbs up and then beckons for us to come inside.

Archie and I lean in towards each other for one last beautiful hug.

Before all this, I imagined myself getting lost in his arms. In him. But I don't feel lost in Archie de Souza's arms anymore.

I feel found.